RUNNING FROM DANGER

Pregnant and alone, Rebecca flees to the US in a bid to escape her ex and his ties to organised crime. There she meets Sheriff Will Hayes in a small backwater town — but can she trust him? When she tries to make a run for it, Will stops her and suggests a plan that involves them both. But Rebecca is unsure of his feelings for her. Can Will keep her safe from her ex and his crime-boss father? Or will the biggest risk come from falling in love?

SARAH PURDUE

RUNNING
FROM
DANGER

Complete and Unabridged

LINFORD
Leicester

First published in Great Britain in 2018

First Linford Edition
published 2019

A catalogue record for this book is available
from the British Library.

ISBN 978–1–4448–4229–6

Published by
F. A. Thorpe (Publishing)
Anstey, Leicestershire

Set by Words & Graphics Ltd.
Anstey, Leicestershire
Printed and bound in Great Britain by
T. J. International Ltd., Padstow, Cornwall

This book is printed on acid-free paper

1

The blue flashing lights, reflected in Rebecca's rear-view mirror, were hard to ignore. She had slowed down in the hope that the police car just wanted to overtake her. She had been driving carefully, and not used to driving on what she considered to be the wrong side of the road, she was probably driving too slowly.

But no. The police car didn't attempt to pass her, not even when the windy road straightened out for a section. The message was clear. Whoever was driving the police car wanted her to pull over . . . and that was the last thing she wanted to do.

The whine of the siren was suddenly added to the lights and made her jump in her seat. She knew she couldn't stall any longer.

She pulled her rented car into one of

the many parking spots that were used by tourists to admire the mountain views. A glimpse in her side mirror told her that the police car had followed suit and a man in a Sheriff's uniform climbed out, pulling his tan hat on to his head and ensuring it was settled in place. He walked towards Rebecca's car and she pressed the button to make the window lower.

'Ma'am,' the Sheriff said tipping his hat. 'Where you aware that you were crossing the central line?'

Rebecca looked up and blinked. The Sheriff was younger than she had expected, probably not much older than her, maybe thirty. He had a rugged look about him that seemed suited to an outdoor life, and piercing blue eyes.

'Was I?' Rebecca said. 'I'm sorry I'm still getting used to driving on the right. I thought I was being so careful,' she added.

The Sheriff locked eyes with her for a second and then pulled his gaze away to inspect her car.

'Ma'am, please step out of the vehicle.'

Rebecca did her best to hide her sigh.

This was not supposed to be happening. She was only a few miles away from the place that she intended to call home, at least for a while, and the last thing she needed was to be brought to the attention of the local police.

It did seem unfair; she had watched her speed and been careful at junctions. With a small shake of the head she pushed open her door and slid her legs out. Grasping hold of the handle above the car door she levered herself up.

The Sheriff was not watching her climb out of the car. Instead he seemed to be doing a disapproving inspection of the car, checking the tyres with a booted kick.

Rebecca stood where she was and waited for him to finish. It all seemed a little unnecessary. The car was less than a year old and was clearly displaying the rental company sticker, but she supposed there wasn't much for a Sheriff to do with his time in a small town like Blowing Rock.

'Ma'am, I'm going to need to conduct a sobriety test,' the Sheriff said and finally he looked up. Rebecca stood with her hands on her hips, making no attempt to hide her growing belly.

'I can assure you I haven't been drinking,' she said with one eyebrow raised.

The Sheriff seemed unable to drag his eyes away from her midriff, or what was left of it after seven months of pregnancy, but then he seemed to remember himself and hurriedly looked up.

'I'm sure you haven't,' he said. 'But I'd still like you to stand there and walk in a straight line for me. When you've walked ten paces, please turn and walk back.'

Rebecca was tempted to argue, but she wanted to get away more than to point out the ridiculousness of the situation. Of course, she hadn't been drinking. For one thing it wasn't even ten o'clock in the morning, and for another she was clearly expecting a baby. But this guy was clearly a 'jobsworth' and the best thing she could do was play along with the charade.

Making an effort to hide her feelings, she walked as directed, turned and walked back.

'Good. Now stand here and look to one side.'

Rebecca did as she was told, wondering if he was now just messing with her.

'That's fine. Now I need you to stand on one leg and maintain your balance.'

Rebecca raised her chin. Balance wasn't easy for a woman whose centre of gravity had been so altered by her blooming belly and she was glad that she had managed to do her pregnancy yoga, despite all the things going on in her life.

She lifted her right leg off the ground, resisting the urge to demonstrate the tree pose, and looked him levelly in the eye. To her surprise he gazed back, without showing an inch of shame at making her try and balance on one leg.

'I'm pleased to say you've passed.'

'Well, I haven't been drinking so I'm not surprised.' Rebecca's words came out a little more sharply than she intended.

'If I might see you driver's licence and insurance documents?' he asked. Rebecca lent into the car for her bag and pulled both out.

It seemed that his politeness increased as hers deteriorated, which was kind of infuriating.

'Here you are, officer.'

'Sheriff,' the man said, 'Sheriff Hayes.'

Rebecca nodded, worried that whatever she said might make the situation worse.

'You're from England?' Hayes asked as he scanned her driver's licence.

'Yes. I'm going to be staying in my grandfather's place, at least until I get settled.'

'The old Williams place?'

Rebecca blinked in surprised and Hayes laughed. It was a warm, rich sound and strangely comforting, despite the circumstances.

'Everyone knows everyone round here. Mike, the caretaker, told me that some of the family were going to come and stay.'

'Oh,' Rebecca said.

That was not really what she was hoping for. She had known that turning up in a small American town as an obviously English woman — particularly one who was pregnant — was going to draw some attention but she had hoped that she might be able to slip quietly into the life and quickly be unworthy of notice, since that was what she needed to avoid more than anything.

'Do you know where you're going?' Sheriff Hayes asked. Rebecca jumped just a little — she had almost forgotten he was there.

'I should be fine,' she said, which wasn't exactly true. She had a map but she also knew that the property was off one of the side roads, up in the mountains.

'Well, how about you follow me?'

'I couldn't possibly put you out like that.'

'You wouldn't be, Mrs Buckingham. Besides, that's how we do things round here.'

Rebecca didn't correct him about her name. Although she had planned to go by Williams, her mother's maiden name and the name on the deeds to the cabin, perhaps it would go better if everyone believed she was married.

'We have tourists getting lost out here all the time, and as my Uncle Bob likes to say, prevention is better than cure.'

Sheriff Hayes seemed to have turned up his accent to full-blown country folk and Rebecca wasn't sure what to make of it.

'Well, if you really don't mind, that would be very helpful.'

'Follow me, ma'am,' he said tipping his hat.

Rebecca stared after him as he walked back to his car emblazoned with Caldwell and Watauga County Sheriff's Department.

She wasn't surprised. Based on her grandfather's stories, this part of the world was turning out exactly as she had imagined it would. The contrast to life in London was vast, but she was glad of it.

She walked back to her own car and did the awkward shuffle that enabled her to squeeze behind the steering wheel. It was getting harder as her tummy swelled, and she wondered if she would ever get to a point where her arms wouldn't be able to reach at all. If that was the case, she might need to find herself a place in town so that she could walk everywhere.

She shook her head and reminded herself of her new mantra: *one step at a time*.

Sheriff Hayes had been waiting patiently for her and as she turned her key, he slipped his car back out on the road.

Was it her imagination or was he making a show of driving close to the side, as if he thought she might need a lesson in driving on American roads? She rolled her eyes, glancing at herself in the rear-view mirror as she did so, but all the time making sure to drive in his wake.

Two miles down the road, Hayes slowed down, indicating left. Rebecca followed him up a road that quickly became a dirt track — and then not even that.

Rebecca had seen the photographs but never actually been to the cabin. She had inherited it from her maternal grandfather when she was a teenager, and her parents had arranged for it to be rented out to tourists to cover its upkeep and to bring in some money to help with Rebecca's university bills. There had never been any talk of visiting it and so Rebecca had never really thought about doing so, until now.

Sheriff Hayes had slowed right down. His car seemed to have no trouble negotiating the pitted roadway, but Rebecca felt as if she was being thrown around in her seat — and her baby was not happy about it. She placed a hand on her belly and rubbed it gently.

'It's OK, little one, we're nearly there. I'll get us a vehicle more suited to the terrain as soon as I can, but soon we'll be tucked up safe and sound in Grandad's cabin.'

Then suddenly they had arrived.

The cabin looked well cared-for, which was a relief. Rebecca wanted to get away but she wasn't exactly a hardy, live-off-the-land kind of person. It was single-storey and had a metal chimney that was smoking, suggesting that Mike had left the fire going, as promised. The outside had a wraparound porch with rustic furniture and swing seat. It all looked old but well-maintained, and Rebecca knew she had Mike to thank for that.

Rebecca's door opened and a hand was offered. She took it, since to do otherwise would seem churlish, and if she was honest she needed help to free herself from the confines of the car.

'Mike left the key in the usual spot.'

Rebecca nodded and walked up the wooden steps to the front door. The key was hanging on a hook, obvious for all the world to see — not that she could imagine much of the world ever finding itself this far off the beaten track. That was the hope, anyway. She had to stand on tiptoe to reach and wondered why the Sheriff hadn't dashed up to help her — that seemed to be his modus operandi — but a glance over her shoulder told her that he was busy unloading her luggage from the boot of the car.

The key turned with ease and Rebecca pushed the door open.

The kitchen and lounge were one large room, filled with comfortable furniture and two wood-burning stoves. A huge log store took up one wall, full to the brim so at least she wouldn't have to worry about that in the near future. The sun was shining outside, but autumn was turning the leaves gold and she knew that cold weather would be nipping at her heels soon enough.

There were three doors; two led to bedrooms, and one to the bathroom, which was not luxurious but certainly functional.

'Where do you want your luggage?' Hayes asked from the doorway.

Rebecca turned from her inspection of her new home. 'There's just fine, thank you. I appreciate the help.' Although she didn't like admitting it, she did. It had certainly made this part of her journey a little easier.

'No problem, ma'am. I think you'll find us a friendly town. There's no phone up here and you won't get a cell phone signal, but after the trouble a while back, Mike fitted a radio. Just press the button and you'll get straight through to the Sheriff's station.'

Rebecca dimly remembered Mike emailing her something about a party of 'towners' as he called them who got themselves entangled with some poison oak and became in need of urgent medical attention.

'That's good,' Rebecca said, although she wasn't sure if it was.

She had ditched her mobile phone and had no intention of emailing anyone. That was the point of being here, after all. But perhaps a connection to the outside world would be a good thing, particular when she neared her due date.

'The stove's good to go, just keep feeding her wood and you won't ever need to re-light her,' Hayes said, closing the metal door on the old range and nodding in approval. 'Mike said he got you the basics, but you'd be welcome to come in to town to grab a bite to eat. Most of us meet at Peggy's around six for supper.'

'That's very kind of you, but it's been a long trip and I think all I really want is an early night.'

'Of course. Well, just know that you'd be welcome anytime.'

Hayes sounded a little bemused, as if his offer was rarely refused.

'Our doctor's office is off the main street. Ask anyone and they'll be sure to point you in the right direction,' he added as he opened the door, turning and glancing at her belly.

Rebecca folded her arms across it.

'Thank you. I'll make sure I come to town in the next few days.'

'If you want to find somewhere more suitable to stay then Miss Joyce is our local realtor. I'm sure she could find you something better for a lady in your condition.'

Sheriff Hayes tipped his hat one more time and then he was out the door.

Rebecca glared at his retreating back.

Why did people — men in particular — think that because you were pregnant you weren't capable of looking after yourself?

She turned the key in the lock behind him. She didn't want any unwelcome visitors. It didn't mean she was afraid, it was simply a sensible precaution, she told herself — one that anyone would take, even Sheriff Hayes, had he known what she did.

Rebecca stared at the door. There

were no bolts or additional locks, something she would have to ask Mike to rectify. Hopefully he would do so discreetly — she didn't think she wanted to give Sheriff Hayes the satisfaction of knowing that she wanted more security. No doubt he would consider it more evidence that this cabin in the woods was no place for a 'lady in her condition'.

Satisfied the door was firmly locked, she made her way around the rest of the cabin, checking all the windows and the back door. Once she was certain they were as secure as they could be for now, she filled the kettle with water and placed it on the hot plate of the stove.

What she needed was some camomile tea and something to eat. Maybe then she would find the energy to unpack. That was all she needed to do; unpack and figure out how she was going to keep herself and her baby safe.

2

According to her watch it wasn't yet six o'clock in the evening, but to Rebecca it seemed more as if it was six in the morning following a night which had not involved any sleep.

She had unpacked her two suitcases, which having been packed in a hurry contained only the basics. She would need to find a local shopping centre in the next week or so, but for now she would make do with the clothes and bits and pieces she had managed to bring with her.

Although she had never visited the cabin before, she could almost feel her grandfather's presence. He had lived here as a boy, all the way through to the time that he had emigrated to the UK to live with his only daughter. He had always seemed a little sad to Rebecca's teenage eyes, but then he *had* just lost his wife of fifty years and left behind everything he had known.

Now it made sense to her and she could only wish she had understood better, back then.

Moving halfway across the world to the tiny retirement flat in the small Kent seaside town from this cabin in the woods must have been a complete culture shock.

What she had seen on her drive to the cabin had been mountain ranges and wide blue skies, with trees as far as the eye can see, and not many people. So different to the bustling, slightly jaded and run-down town of her childhood.

She could see now why he had loved this place so much. It was starting to feel like home already, even with just the few things that she had brought with her.

She had put the book she was reading on the bedside table in the room she had claimed as her own, and the small china ring dish that had been a gift from her grandmother was now on the kitchen countertop, where she could drop her rings while she cooked. She hadn't brought any photographs with her; her memories of those she loved would have to do.

There was no television in the cabin but there was a small radio. Rebecca turned it on, but it only seemed capable of picking up the local radio. Nevertheless, the country music and local news were just the back ground noise she needed. She didn't want to feel lonely, even though all of this was down to her. It had been her decision and now she needed to live with it.

Her belly fluttered as her baby moved and she placed a reassuring hand across the spot.

'We'll be OK,' she said softly. 'Just you wait and see. Mummy's got this.'

She yawned and stretched. Maybe she should sit down for a minute. Her ankles were starting to swell and her shoes felt tight. She kicked them off and settled on to the sofa, pulling the throw, which had been artfully laid across the back, down across her legs and closed her eyes.

She would rest for a couple of minutes and then find something to do to carry her through to bedtime. She wanted to get her body clock adjusted as soon as she could.

★   ★   ★

Something was happening, something bad. Rebecca didn't know what it was. Or where she was. But it was bad. She had to get away. Escape.

Heart pounding, she tried to get her legs to move, but she couldn't. A heavy weight seemed to have been strapped across them. She kicked. Tried to free herself. Used her arms to try and pull herself up. It was no use. She was trapped.

She opened her mouth to scream. No sound came. She needed to open her eyes. It was a nightmare. If she could just see where she was, everything would be OK . . .

Rebecca's eyes suddenly snapped open. She felt as if she had reached the surface of a deep pool, taking that first, big deep breath.

There was no light; a darkness that was complete surrounded her. She looked around frantically, and then realised she was in the cabin. Her arms were free, but she still couldn't move her legs. She reached down, tried to feel what was holding her in place.

Her hands touched fur and her ears were filled with a deep, rumbling growl . . . Rebecca froze.

This was the mountains, this was America. They had bears and wolves and other things that might want to eat a person!

Despite everything that had happened, she had a deep desire to be back home, where the most dangerous animal was her neighbour's semi-feral cat, ingloriously misnamed Cuddles as if in some vain attempt to soften his terrifying personality.

The weight shifted as Rebecca tried to stay still. Her thoughts went to the radio that Sheriff Hayes had said would connect her directly with the Sheriff station. She had no idea if it were even manned at night, but right now she would welcome Sheriff Hayes and all his disapproving 'this is no place for a pregnant lady' talk.

However, it was on a handmade shelf in the kitchen, so she would need to free herself.

Gingerly she felt down her legs again, trying to keep her shaking hands still. *Show no fear.* That's what her grandfather had always said about animals. It sounded so simple when you were sitting in a conservatory looking out at manicured gardens, where the fiercest creature you were likely to meet was a squirrel.

'Easy, boy,' she found herself saying as her hands made contact again. Whatever it was, it had long fur and she could also make out a thick tail. It was too large for a cat . . . maybe a bobcat?

Did they have those in North Carolina? At least it wasn't a bear, not a full-grown one anyway.

She felt the fur ruffle under her touch and froze. She didn't want to make it angry, but she needed to know what it was — and how dangerous it was. She tried to pull one leg towards her. Perhaps if she could free one leg at a time, she wouldn't disturb it too much. Maybe then she could creep to the radio and call for help?

As she moved her leg, the growling returned, and she willed herself to stay still. The growling seemed to morph into whining and Rebecca frowned. It seemed a familiar sound. She reached out once more and felt the edge of the creature. It was fully on the blanket. Maybe she could lift the blanket edge up and over its head and then she could free herself in the confusion. It wasn't a great plan but short of lying there all night and asking the creature sweetly not to eat her, she hadn't got any better ideas.

She gripped the edge of the blanket in both hands and braced herself, lifting the blanket up and sliding her legs out in one reasonably smooth motion. Her legs were free but it was not easy getting to her feet with so much weight around her middle. The blanket moved beside her and there was the low growling again. With one desperate shove she managed to get to her feet.

With no light to guide her she stumbled around in the dark, arms outstretched and braced to run into something.

Her hands touched the kitchen surface and she remembered that a torch was standing on one edge. She felt along for it, sure the blanket monster had moved, sure it was stalking her.

With shaking hands, she flicked the torch on and a thin line of light appeared. Rebecca shone the light around her but could make out nothing out of place.

The door was shut and the key in place. There was no tell-tale movement of curtains at the windows that might suggest one of them had been broken or forced open. She could detect no movement around her. Finally she focused the beam of light onto the sofa.

The blanket was still there, and it was still moving. Rising and falling slowly, as if the monster was asleep.

Rebecca crept into the kitchen area, looking for something she could use to defend herself.

As quietly as she could she pulled open a drawer. It contained knives and forks, nothing useful. There was a grunt from the sofa and Rebecca grabbed the nearest thing she could from the drawer — an old-fashioned wooden rolling pin. Should she try and tackle the creature herself or call for help?

Calling for help went against her better nature. She was always one to fix her own problems. But there was more than herself to think about these days. She needed to think about the baby.

Her torch trained on the blanket, Rebecca moved across to the shelf with the radio on it. A quick glance told her that it was switched off. She turned her attention back to the blanket. It continued to move slowly up and down. Was it possible that whatever creature had managed to find its way into the cabin had fallen asleep?

For a moment she was tempted to creep across the room and slowly draw the blanket back, to look on the face of her enemy, but the butterflies were back — and not the sort that meant you were scared or nervous, which she was. It was her baby.

She still marvelled at the idea that in two short months she would get to meet him or her. She felt like she knew them already, but somehow the idea that she would get to hold the baby — *her* baby — was nothing short of miraculous.

The gentle reminder was enough. Her old life was over and she was starting the new. Her new life was going to be about much more than just herself. Her baby would always come first.

She made her decision. Keeping any eye on the blanket she reached up and flicked the switch.

The electronic hum seemed so loud in her ears. It felt as if it was reverberating around the room, working up to a crescendo. Rebecca kept her anxious eyes fixed on the blanket. It shuffled a little but then there was a sort of sigh and the rhythmic up and down movement returned.

Rebecca steeled herself and turned away from it, trying to remember what Sheriff Hayes had said. Something about it making a direct link to the Sheriff's station? She could only hope that she had remembered correctly.

She lifted the small black handset and moved it close to her lips. She had no idea what the correct radio speak was.

'Hello?' she said softly. There was no reply. Surely there should be the noise of static. Holding the torch in her free hand, she shone it on the handset. On one side was a slim button. She pressed it and tried again. 'Hello?'

This time she was rewarded with

static, but then there was silence.

'Hello? Can anyone hear me?' She spoke louder this time, flicking her eyes in direction of the sofa and praying that her words wouldn't disturb the animal. There was no static and then she realised she was holding the button down. She released her grip and the radio burst into life.

'This is Sheriff Hayes. Who is this?'

'Rebecca, Rebecca Buckingham.'

'Mrs Buckingham, you do realise that it's three in the morning?' He didn't sound like he was asleep, but it was hard to tell if he was annoyed or not, his voice sounding tinny coming out of the small box.

'It's an emergency!' she hissed urgently. Why had he told her to call if he was going to behave like this when she did?

'What's the problem?'

He didn't sound overly concerned. He probably thought she was making a fuss about nothing. For a second she wished she had crossed the room and revealed the face of the monster. But then her free hand drifted to her belly. However much she wanted to, now was not the time for heroics. She had more than herself to think about.

'Something has got into the cabin.'

'What kind of something?' He at least sounded a little more interested now.

'I don't know! It's big and furry and it growls.'

'Where is it?'

'In the lounge, on the sofa.'

There was a pause and Rebecca felt herself blush. It wasn't as if it could be a bear. Was she just making a fuss? The blanket shifted and she let out a little yelp.

'Can you get to one of the bedrooms?'

'I think so.'

'Close the door and move furniture against it if you have to. I'm on my way. Don't come out till I tell you the coast is clear.'

'OK,' Rebecca said, her voice shaking.

She was tired and scared and although she would never admit it, she was relieved that someone was coming — even if that someone was Sheriff Hayes. Right now she would even accept the inevitable lecture on why cabins in the woods were no place for pregnant women on their own. If she was honest, she was wondering whether he might be right.

She placed the handset back onto the metal box, with one eye fixed on the sofa. The handset slipped off and crashed on to the work surface. Rebecca didn't wait for a response from the creature, but just ran as fast as she could to the nearest room and slammed the door.

Leaning all her weight against it she prayed the journey from the Sheriff's station to the cabin wouldn't take long.

3

Rebecca was in the bathroom, which was great if she needed to use the facilities, but not so great in terms of finding anything she could use to barricade herself inside.

So instead she sat on the floor, with her back to the door and her feet braced against the bath tub, and listened.

The cabin seemed eerily quiet, but she could still imagine the beast prowling around the room, sniffing out its prey. She strained her ears to listen out for the sound of the Sheriff's car driving up the pitted lane.

She had no watch, so no idea what time it was, or how long it had been since she had called him. He would come though, wouldn't he? He didn't seem like the kind of man who would leave a damsel in distress, even one who had stubbornly put herself in the situation she need rescuing from against his advice.

The bathroom was cold. There was no source of heat in here and with the door closed, none of the heat from the wood-burning stove could filter in. She shivered, still dressed in her maternity jeans and a cotton top.

She wrapped her arms around her belly. She doubted the baby would be affected by the cold but somehow it did make her feel better and she hoped the baby would feel the love she had for it. She was desperate to keep the sex of the baby a surprise; she wanted to do it old school, but somehow calling the baby 'it' seemed wrong.

'I hope you understand,' she whispered softly.

Rebecca felt a gentle ripple under her hand and she took that as a sign that the baby was on board with the surprise plan.

'It's going to be OK,' she added, probably more for herself than the baby.

There was noise from the front of the cabin. The sound of tyres on an uneven muddy surface, a car door slammed and footsteps on the wooden steps, then a key being inserted.

Rebecca closed her eyes; she had left her key in the door. Sheriff Hayes wouldn't be able to get in. She shifted, so that she was facing the door. Should she make a run for the front door? Perhaps she could get it unlocked before the creature got to her? Her heart was pounding in her chest. She had to do something.

She couldn't just sit there. She shifted again, so that she had room to crack open the bathroom door. She would take a peek and then decide what to do.

The lump covered by blanket on the sofa seemed unbothered by the sound of the car drawing up or the footsteps outside. Rebecca had no idea if this was a good thing or not but she got to her feet as quietly as she could.

Pulling the door back, she charged

into the main room of the cabin.

The front door burst open and Rebecca skidded to a halt! The door was now hanging off the top hinge and the door jamb had split, sending splinters of wood across the floor.

Rebecca locked eyes with Sheriff Hayes, who had entered the cabin with a shotgun and then spun to stare at the sofa.

A head was now resting on the sofa back and two eyes looked at her balefully.

Before Rebecca's terrified brain could process what she was looking at, Sheriff Hayes had stepped in front of her and was holding the shotgun steadily, pointing at the creature.

Rebecca took a sideways step. She could see now what the creature was. It looked back at her, head now on one side, as if it was trying to work out what on earth was going on.

'It's just a dog!' Rebecca said, feeling both relieved and embarrassed all at the same time.

'Stay back,' Hayes warned, nevertheless. 'It might have rabies.'

'Looks in good health to me,' Rebecca said.

The dog yawned, completed a complicated stretch that a yogi would have been proud of, and jumped off the sofa. He trotted across the floor and sat next to Rebecca, leaning against her leg. She reached down and ruffled the dog's head.

Hayes took hold of Rebecca's arm and gently pulled her away. The dog whined but stayed where he was as Hayes got to his knees and proceeded to do a full check.

'No tag or collar. He might be microchipped. I'll take him with me and get Andi to take a look at him.'

'Andi?' Rebecca said, suddenly worried that the dog was going to end up in the pound — or worse.

'Our vet.' He turned to look up at her. 'She's Scottish. I think you'll like her.'

Rebecca nearly laughed. There was something about Americans who seemed to think that anyone from an island as small as Great Britain must know each other and even if they didn't, they were bound to get on.

'What will happen to him?' she asked, moving back over the room and stooping down to ruffle the dog behind his ears. It was obviously the perfect spot, because he went slightly cross-eyed and his tongue lolled out of his mouth happily.

'If we can find his owner, we'll reunite them.'

'And if not?'

Hayes shrugged and Rebecca didn't like it.

'Please tell Andi that if you can't find an owner then I'll take him.'

Hayes looked at her with barely concealed surprise. 'I didn't realise you were planning to stay that long.'

'I'm not sure, but wherever I end up I can take him with me.'

'What about your husband?'

'I don't have one,' Rebecca replied dryly.

It wasn't going to be possible to keep that secret for long, she knew, so she might as well let Hayes tell the rest of the town.

'Oh, sorry . . . I mean your partner?'

'I don't have one of those either. It's just me and Bump here.'

'Oh. Right,' Hayes said and Rebecca couldn't tell if he was shocked, appalled, or something else entirely.

He stood up quickly and Rebecca got the impression that he wanted to get out of there as soon as possible.

He looked towards the door and Rebecca followed his gaze. She couldn't really be angry. She had called him, after all — and she was the one who had left the key in the lock.

'I'm sure Mike will be able to fix it,' she said, feeling a little deflated at the sight.

'Well, you can't stay here with the door off its hinges. Anything might make its way in.'

Rebecca couldn't see his face, since it was turned away inspecting the door, but she had the distinct feeling that he was having an amused dig at her overreaction to discovering a stray dog in her cabin. 'You'll have to come stay with me.'

It was said in the no-nonsense tone that most officers of the law had mastered. Rebecca suspected it was necessary in that line of work but that wasn't to say that she appreciated it being used on her.

'I'm sure we can manoeuvre the door into place. The sun will be up soon.' That was a pure guess on her part, since she had no real idea.

'I can't leave you here like this. I'll take you into town and get you a place to stay and then I'll come back and fix the door.'

'You don't need to do that,' Rebecca said, feeling that Hayes was making an embarrassing situation even worse. 'I called you up here, which now seems completely ridiculous, and I fell asleep with the key in the door. You wouldn't have needed to break in if none of that had happened. I couldn't possibly expect you to — '

Hayes cut her off with a wave of his hand. 'I used to be in Army, so I've had a lot of training in fixing things and I insist.'

'Well at least let me pay you,' Rebecca said thinking of her small pot of money that could really do without unnecessary expenses.

'I won't hear of it. But if you like, you could buy me breakfast. Peggy should be opening up by the time we get into town.'

'It's a deal.'

Rebecca wondered what kind of deal she had got herself into. She wanted to get to know people, but she didn't want to get close to anyone — she couldn't afford to — but it would be lonely here without having at least a few people she could say hello to. And as time went on and things settled, she wanted the baby to have friends and people in their lives who would love him or her.

The Sheriff didn't seem like the

wisest place to start but then she didn't have much in the way of a choice.

'I'll load our furry friend in the car, if you need a minute?'

Rebecca wasn't sure if he was implying that she needed to tidy herself up. There was no doubt in her mind that she did. She had travelled in her clothes and then slept in them on the sofa — and that was all before crawling around on the bathroom floor! She must have looked a state.

Perhaps Hayes was right and she should think about booking into a motel for a couple of nights until the door was sorted. Before she could change her mind, she grabbed her carry-on case and filled it with everything she might need.

Hayes was waiting for her in the main room and quickly relieved her of the suitcase. She thought about protesting, it wasn't as if it was heavy, but something about his manner told her it would be a waste of time and energy to argue — and she was definitely short on energy.

'I'm glad to see you're taking my

advice,' he said seriously as he loaded her small suitcase into the boot of his Sheriff's vehicle.

Rebecca climbed into the front passenger seat. She had, but she didn't want to tell him that — and she wasn't sure why.

'I thought I might take a motel room for a couple of nights, just until the door is sorted,' Rebecca said by way of a reply which was not, she hoped, openly agreeing with his statement.

'The motels are all out on the interstate but Peggy has a few rooms behind the diner that she rents out.'

'I'll only need a couple of nights,' Rebecca said, feeling like she needed to point this out.

'Peggy's flexible for the right person. Besides, I think you'll like living in town.'

Rebecca turned her gaze to look out of the window.

She could feel herself getting frustrated and she didn't want to speak out of turn. Sheriff Hayes was perfectly entitled to his opinion, but she was going back to the cabin once the door was fixed, and she wasn't going to be dissuaded.

She didn't want to be rude — he was going to fix the door and was driving her into town — but she needed to feel hidden away, and she couldn't imagine that would be the case if she stayed at Peggy's diner.

The road was narrow and wound through the woods, which seemed to cling to the side of the mountains in short ribbons. It was still dark, so she couldn't see the view, but every now and then when the car took a particularly sharp bend, its headlights would spill out to the right and she could make out the mountain ranges which would flash into view and then out again.

It was certainly spectacular and Rebecca planned to explore the area once she worked out what she was going to do next.

At least she knew what she *wasn't* going to do. She wasn't going to stay in town, not for longer than she needed to. Until things quietened down she needed to be out of sight — out of sight of anyone who might get curious as to why she was there.

4

The *Welcome to Blowing Rock* sign was lit up by an old fashioned light and announced proudly that the population was one thousand, three hundred and six.

Shortly to be one thousand, three hundred and seven, Rebecca thought — *and then eight.*

She looked down and smiled at the thought of her baby's arrival. It was still a surprise when she looked down and saw her growing belly. It had taken a while to get her head around the idea that she was having a baby, but now her body was showing her and making her aware every minute of the day.

Sheriff Hayes slowed the car as they had passed the welcome sign and the road seemed to straighten out as they reached the first signs of civilisation. First a house appeared, all made of wood and painted pale blue, surrounded by a grass front garden and flag pole proudly displaying the American flag. It was exactly what Rebecca had imagined this place would be like.

The houses appeared more regularly now, but not one looked exactly like another. It was so unlike home, where housing estates seemed to be springing up everywhere — rows of houses with impossibly small gardens, whose only mission in life appeared to be to look exactly like their neighbours. These houses had character; they had been personalised and seemed to have life in their wooden walls.

Perhaps when the baby came, she could find one she could rent. Just the thought of rent made a shiver run through her. There were so many things to think about, to worry about — and money was only one of them.

Hayes moved his hand to the dash and she realised he was turning up the heat.

'You should have said if you were

cold,' he said, sounding as if he were chiding himself more than her. 'I'm used to the weather hereabouts, so I often-time forget.'

'I'm fine,' Rebecca said smiling at him. He had been so kind and really had nothing to berate himself about, except perhaps his attitude to a woman's ability to cope on her own. 'I think I'll need to go and buy some more appropriate clothes, though.'

'There are a couple of places in town. I can show you once you're settled.'

Rebecca looked at him with slight suspicion. Surely a Sheriff had more to do than give her the guided tour?

'I'm sure you have work to do.' *And my door to fix*, she thought to herself.

'No, it's my day off.'

Rebecca's eyes widened in horror.

'I'm so sorry, I would never . . . ' She didn't finish the sentence.

The whole situation only seemed to get worse. First she had called him out, hysterical about a dog — not that she knew it was a dog at the time — that had somehow made its way into the cabin, and now she was keeping him from his day off.

'Don't worry. Since I'm the only Sheriff, my day off is only nominal. If there's a problem, I'm on duty.' He smiled but kept his eyes on the road.

The sun was making an orange glow appear on the horizon and it seemed like the people of Blowing Rock were starting to get about their daily business.

'Wow, that's . . . ' Rebecca couldn't think of a word for his sense of duty other than ' . . . noble'.

'It's the job. When I was in the Army I worked for months without any downtime, so this is basically a luxury.'

Rebecca looked to see if he was joking but he looked serious.

'Besides, this isn't the kind of place that's exactly a hotbed of crime.'

He grinned now, and Rebecca could see how much he loved his town. She was a little envious. More than anything she wanted to belong somewhere, to feel like she had a home, somewhere she could feel safe. But the truth was she wasn't sure how long she would be able to stay, how long it would be safe.

Hayes turned the car onto what appeared to be the main road. On one side there were independent shops. Out the front was a wide pavement and then car parking spaces where cars could park at an angle. On the other side of the road was a green space. Rebecca could make out a children's play area and various benches and a few wooden picnic tables as well as a small wooden hut that looked like it might sell ice cream when the weather was warm enough.

It seemed idyllic and, not for the first time, she hoped she might be able to find a way to stay.

Hayes pulled the car in at an angle and Rebecca got her first view of Peggy's.

It looked like a diner that had been there for decades and had remained unchanged. The neon sign that hung in the window advertised hamburgers and milkshakes and the fact that the diner was open for business.

Hayes had climbed out of the car and walked around to open Rebecca's door before she had time to do it for herself. Once again, he offered her his hand and she took it. Better to receive help than look foolish trying to climb out.

Hayes walked across to the diner door and held it open for Rebecca. There was a burst of heat and sound as Rebecca walked through.

Inside was exactly how she imagined a retro diner might look. The seating arrangements were all booths with shiny tables. There was a long bar across the back room, with stools for those dining alone, and behind this was a long, narrow kitchen. The walls were covered in black and white tiles and hung with neon lit signs advertising various cold drinks.

Hayes directed her to one of the booths that meant they would have a view of main street. A couple sat in the booth next to theirs and both smiled up at Rebecca as if they weren't surprised to see her there. Perhaps news really did travel fast in small towns? Rebecca smiled back and took her seat. Thankfully there was enough room for her and her bump.

Hayes handed her a menu as an older lady, dressed in 1950s style, appeared with a pad and pen in hand.

'Will — I wasn't expecting to see you this early on your day off!' The older woman turned to Rebecca and crinkled her eyes up in a smile. 'And you must be Mr Williams' granddaughter,' she said to Rebecca, who returned her smile, thinking how different it was here to London, where no one smiled unless they were slightly unhinged!

'And would I be right in guessing you are the famous Peggy?' Rebecca said and was rewarded with another beaming smile.

'That would be me. I remember your grandpa. He used to come in here when my daddy ran the place. I was only a little girl, but he was always one to tell me stories of his life in the woods.'

Rebecca laughed, having heard a fair few of those tales herself.

'And I'd be right in thinking he told you them too. I was mighty sorry to hear he had passed.'

Rebecca's smile dropped. He had died many years ago, but she wished now, more than ever, that he was still alive. She wished they could have made this trip to his home together.

'Well now, look at what I've gone and done,' Peggy said, frowning at herself. 'You've only just arrived, probably hankering after something to eat and drink, and here I am just bringing up sad memories.'

'Actually, I'd love to hear more about him when he was younger. I hardly saw him until he moved to the UK.'

'Then I'll be sure to tell you all about it sometime,' Peggy said. 'Now, what can I get you? If you're anything like me when I was carrying mine, you'll be craving for pancakes.'

Rebecca only need to think about this idea for a second before she realised it was exactly what she fancied. 'Perfect,' she said with a smile.

'I'll bring you some orange juice too, you'll be needing your vitamins. And what can I get you Will — your usual?'

Rebecca looked at Hayes, realising that up until now, she hadn't known his first name. Will seemed to suit him.

'Please, Peggy, and then I was hoping you might be able to join us for a quick coffee. Rebecca here has something to ask you.'

'I'm sure Earl can cover for me for ten minutes,' she replied, and bustled away.

Will's attention turned back to Rebecca and she gave him her best *What on earth?* look.

'You need somewhere to stay,' Will said, looking confused.

'I do but I thought you were going to ask. I've only just met Peggy. Don't you think it's a bit forward of me to ask for a favour straight off?'

Will stared at her and then his face broke into a grin as he shook his head. 'Has anyone ever told you how English you are?'

Rebecca raised an eyebrow. 'It never really came up, you know, in England.'

She was feeling a little out of step with her new world and Will has not helping in that regard.

'Well, don't worry, in this town we look after our own and strangers alike. Not that you're a stranger — being related to old Mr Williams means you're practically family.'

Peggy returned with a tray of coffee and orange juice, then she shuffled onto the seat next to Will, who moved up to make room.

'Now then, Rebecca, what is it you need?'

Rebecca blinked. Will did seem to know the town folk — they certainly were straight talkers.

'I've had some . . . issues with the door of the cabin,' Rebecca started to say, wondering how to bring the subject up. She saw Will shift in his seat and his eyes seemed to be telling her to get on with it. 'You see, I feel asleep on the sofa and then when I woke up . . . '

Will made a show of looking at his watch before he butted in with, 'A stray dog got into the cabin. Rebecca didn't know what it was so she called me on the radio. I had to kick the door down as the key had been left in the lock. So Rebecca here needs a place to stay while I sort the door repairs and I said I thought you would be able to help her out.'

Rebecca winced. Hearing the story told out loud made her feel even more foolish, if that was possible.

'I woke up in the dark to find the dog asleep on my legs, but I didn't know what sort of animal it was. It was under the blanket, you see . . . '

Peggy reached over and squeezed Rebecca's hand. 'Only Will here would think that a strange animal in a strange cabin might not be terrifying.'

Peggy's tone was slightly chiding and

Will looked down at the table as if he had been thoroughly told off.

'Poor you. That's not what you need after hours of travel, especially in your condition. Do we know whose the dog is?'

She directed the last comment to Will.

'No, ma'am. He seems friendly enough but no tags. I'll take him to Andi when surgery's over.'

'Remember to tell her that I'll take him if she can't find the owner.'

Peggy looked at her with assessing eyes.

'I wouldn't like for him to have to be put to sleep or anything.' Rebecca felt like she needed to explain why, having been in the country for slightly less than twenty-four hours, she was willing to take on a pet.

Peggy's face broke into a smile and she nodded with approval. 'I have a little holiday let out back,' she said. 'It's small, mind, but I think it should suit you perfectly.'

'You must tell me how much you

usually earn from tourists.'

Peggy shook her head. 'We don't get much in the way of tourists at this time of the year. It usually stands empty all winter, so you'd be doing me a favour keeping it all up together.'

Rebecca frowned; she couldn't take money for nothing, which is what it felt like. She was going to need to make her own way, and the sooner she started the better.

'I'm sure I'll think of something you can do to pay your keep, if you insist.' Peggy's eyes twinkled and Rebecca had a distinct feeling that whatever it was, it unlikely to involve her paying her way with money.

'Well, hopefully it won't take too long to get the door fixed, and then I'll be out of your hair.'

'There's no rush,' Peggy said mildly.

Will looked supremely pleased with himself and Rebecca got the feeling he had found himself an ally on the 'cabins in the woods are no place for pregnant ladies' front.

'Now you eat your breakfast,' Peggy said as an old-fashioned bell rang in the kitchen. 'Once you're done, I'll show you to your new home.'

'Thank you. You're very kind,' Rebecca said with a grateful smile, which was returned.

Peggy got up and walked over to the kitchen, before returning with plates loaded with food. Rebecca's stomach growled in appreciation and her eyes went wide at the stack of pancakes and piles of strawberries that came with it.

'Told you it was the best place in town to eat,' Will said, picking up his fork and tucking in to his pile of bacon, sausages and scrambled eggs.

'We're the only place open this early,' Peggy said as she cleared the table that the other couple had just vacated.

Twenty minutes later Rebecca pushed her plate away. There were a few pancakes left but she was absolutely stuffed.

'That was delicious,' she told Peggy who reappeared to clear their table.

There were more people in the diner

now. Several men sat perched on stools at the bar, one with a newspaper in front of him. Rebecca got the impression that everyone knew everyone else as the conversation seemed to ebb and flow all around the diner.

'Well, if Will here will go and collect your luggage, I can show you to your new home.'

Will wiped his mouth with his napkin and got quickly to his feet. It seemed that what Peggy said was obeyed — and swiftly. Rebecca tried to hide a smile. It seemed funny to her that the local lawman should be so under the thumb of Peggy, the owner of the local diner.

Will quickly reappeared with Rebecca's small suitcase.

'Do you want me to carry it out back?' he asked.

'I think between us we can manage,' Peggy said, rolling her eyes at Rebecca who smiled back. 'Now, hadn't you best be getting that dog off to Andi?'

'Yes, Ma,' he said leaning in and giving her a kiss on the cheek, before pulling out his wallet and placing some notes on the table.

Rebecca reached for her purse, but Will caught the action and waved it away. Breakfast, it seemed, was on him. Rebecca watched him go, wondering how she was going to replay him for all his kindness.

'Will is your son?' Rebecca asked, thinking that Will could have mentioned that fact.

'Not by blood but as near to as you can get without that.' Peggy looked at Rebecca with a smile. 'I married his father after his mother up and left when he was just a baby. She said she felt trapped in such a small town and that she wanted a divorce. Ken was heartbroken, left with a young baby and no wife. I started looking after Wilder when Ken was at work. I'd just come back from college and had no job and then . . . well, eventually we became a little family, I guess.'

Rebecca was processing this — and the fact that Will's name was actually

Wilder — when Peggy picked up Rebecca's suitcase.

'Follow me, sweetheart, and I'll show you around.'

Rebecca slid out from the booth — with a little effort, as it was a bit of a squeeze with her tummy — and followed Peggy, mentally filing away all the new information she had just received about Sheriff Wilder Hayes.

5

The holiday let would suit Rebecca perfectly. It was small and cosy. It had central heating and an ordinary electric stove. There was a small double bedroom, a kitchen, dining, lounge area with all mod cons, and right now they were all very appealing.

And that was a problem; she knew she would be tempted to stay.

She had dumped her small suitcase on the bed and straight away jumped in the shower, before changing into a set of clean clothes.

She was just considering going out to explore and pick up a few basics like milk and tea when there was a knock at the door.

Opening it, she was greeted by a blur of fur and Will. The fur rushed past her, had a quick sniff around and then settled himself on the sofa.

Rebecca laughed and took a step back so that Will could walk in.

'I take it there's no microchip?' Rebecca said.

'No and I've checked, no reports of lost dogs. So he's yours, for now, if you're sure?'

Will was wearing jeans, a T-shirt and lumberjack tartan shirt over the top. He looked younger out of uniform and more like the kind of man you might be friends with . . . or more. Rebecca pushed the thought out of her head. It was ridiculous — for one, she was pregnant with another man's baby, and for another her heart was still broken.

Putting the thought down to jetlag and the overwhelming emotions of the last few days, she turned to Will and tried to focus on anything other than his muscular frame and smiling face.

'Does your mum allow pets?' That was something she had forgotten to ask.

'Sure,' Will said in a way that didn't make it any clearer whether Peggy would or not.

'I would offer you a cup of tea, but I don't have any supplies. I was just about to head out and find a supermarket.'

'I can show you.' Will said, 'You can shop while I take this one for a quick walk.'

Rebecca felt a slight sense of unease. Will was being so friendly and helpful, he couldn't think . . . ? She shook her head. She was being ridiculous. What would he possibly see her in right now? No, this was just the way of small town America, she supposed, and she ought to start getting used to it, without reading something into actions that simply wasn't there.

'That would be lovely, thank you,' she said, picking up her bag.

Thankfully, she had bought some dollars at the airport, which should keep her going for a couple of weeks, but she would need to be careful. It wasn't as if she could access her bank account, not without giving away where she was. She would need to find some kind of work. Hopefully some of the residents of Blowing Rock would be interested in learning French or Italian. Or maybe she could ask Peggy for some work at the diner?

'You OK?' Will asked.

Rebecca blushed as she realised she had left him standing there while she pondered her future.

'Sorry, I was just thinking.' Rebecca forced a smile on to her face. She had made it safely here and that was the most important thing. Everything else she was sure she could sort out.

'You look worried,' Will said. His eyes were fixed on hers and she felt he could read her mind.

'Just lots to think about, that's all,' Rebecca said. She had no intention of sharing her story with anyone. She had no idea how Will would react if she told him, but it felt safer to keep her private life private. From what she knew of him already, she suspected he would want to help and the last thing she wanted to do was draw him into her mess of a life.

'New town and all that.' She smiled up at him, appreciating for the first time how tall he was. His green eyes were watchful but then he smiled too.

'Well, there's plenty folks here who'll be happy to help you.'

'Yes, everyone has been lovely so far.'

Rebecca hurried to the door, to try and hide the colour that was rising up her neck. What a foolish thing to say, since so far the only people she had met from the town were Will and his mum, Peggy.

Will followed, having clipped a lead onto the new collar that the dog was wearing.

'You should probably give him a name,' Will said as he pulled the door closed behind him.

Rebecca turned around for a split second she thought Will was talking about the baby but then realised his attention was focused on the dog.

'Hmm,' Rebecca said. Of all the things she needed to think about right now, naming her temporary, or not so temporary, dog wasn't high on her list.

'How about Goofy? It suits him,' Will said.

Rebecca looked down at the dog who looked like a cross between Lassie and a golden retriever. The dog looked up at her and Rebecca might be kidding herself but he looked as if he were begging her to come up with a different name, any name. She reached down and scratched him behind his ears. 'How about Jack?' she said.

The dog seemed to nod his approval and the name had certainly sent his tail wagging.

'Looks like Jack, it is,' Will said in the kind of way that suggested he thought it was a bit of a boring name for a dog.

Jack barked in response.

'He seems to like it,' Rebecca said as they made their way around the side of the diner and out onto the main street.

'Do you have any names for your baby?'

'I haven't settled on anything yet,' Rebecca said, which wasn't exactly true. They'd had a list of names since the moment they had found out, but Rebecca didn't think she could go with any of them. Not now anyway.

'Do you know what you're having?'

Rebecca shook her head. 'I'd like to be surprised.'

'The doctor's office is over the hardware store. You can't miss it.'

Rebecca smiled in thanks.

She knew she should go for a check-up, but she really needed to find some work first. She knew that healthcare in America would be expensive. Perhaps she should have tried to stay in the UK? Maybe there would have been somewhere she could have gone.

She shook her head. No, this was her best option and she would just have to make it work.

'This is the grocery store,' Will said, somewhat unnecessarily since outside the shop was a long table laden with all ranges of fruit advertised as local produce.

'Thanks,' Rebecca said.

'Ask Bert to bag it up and I'll carry it home. I'll take Jack for a quick run round the park.'

Rebecca opened her mouth to say that he didn't need to, but Will and Jack had already disappeared across the road before she could speak. She stood and watched as Will let Jack off the lead and the dog raced off after a squirrel. She hoped Will would be able to summon him back.

She smiled to herself. She couldn't believe she was worrying about him already. He had only been her temporary responsibility for a few hours.

She turned and walked into the grocery store, collected a mini trolley, and started to walk slowly up and down the aisles. There were a lot of products that were familiar and a whole range that Rebecca only knew about from her grandpa, who had bemoaned the fact that he couldn't get his favourite sweet treats in the UK.

Rebecca selected a few, then forced herself to walk away. The baby needed fruit and vegetables, not junk.

When she reached the single checkout, Will was already waiting for her, chatting to a young woman at the tills. They both looked up as she approached, and Will at least smiled.

'Tash, this is Rebecca,' Will said, and Tash managed a sort of half-hearted smile.

Rebecca got the distinct impression that Tash, who couldn't be more than late teens, had a bit of a thing for the handsome Sheriff — who was probably way too old for her, but woe betide anyone who told her that.

Rebecca picked up a jar of spaghetti sauce and Will started to unload the trolley. She wanted to protest that she was perfectly capable, but it didn't seem worth the argument so she moved to the other end of the checkout.

She helped herself to a brown paper bag from the pile but then a much older man appeared at her side, taking the bag gently from her hands.

'That's my job, little lady,' he said, his eyes twinkling. 'We don't let folk pack their own shopping here.'

'Thank you,' Rebecca said with a

smile, thinking that this must be Bert.

'And if you need it carried out to your car, I do that too,' Bert beamed up at her, reminding her of her grandpa. 'I love your accent,' he added and then looked down shyly to focus on his job.

'I love yours, too,' Rebecca said, sure that Tash was rolling her eyes, but Bert's reaction was enough to make her glad she had said it. His face flushed pink and he looked very pleased.

'I've worked here since I was a lad,' he added.

'Then I guess you must have known my grandfather?'

'Fred was a star football player,' Bert said.

'I didn't know that,' Rebecca said, finding it hard to imagine her grandfather in a varsity jacket.

'There are photos of him up at the school. I could show you,' Bert added hopefully.

'I'd like that,' Rebecca said.

'Have to be another time, Bert. Rebecca needs to get her groceries home,' Will said, but smiling gently at the older man.

'Of course,' Bert said, as if the idea of groceries being left while they galivanted off to the school was a scandalous idea. 'I don't work Thursdays, so you just let me know,' Bert said placing a hand on Rebecca's arm.

'I will, thank you.'

Bert handed the two brown paper bags to Will and Rebecca led the way out of the store.

It might be her imagination, but she was sure she could feel Tash glowering at her back.

Jack's lead was tied to the small metal frame that seemed to serve as a dog park. He had been sitting there happily watching the world go by, but as soon as he saw Rebecca he started leaping up and trying to lick her face as if he hadn't seen her in years.

Rebecca laughed, gently pushed him off her and then knelt down to give him a good stroke.

'We weren't gone that long,' she said

as he reached up and licked her nose.

Rebecca untied his lead and she and Will walked back along the road. It took much longer than their journey to the grocery store as there were more people out and about and each one stopped to say hello and to be introduced to Rebecca. Her face ached with all the smiling and she had no idea how she was going to remember who everyone was, or who was related to whom.

Will laughed when he saw her expression.

'Don't worry, folks won't hold it against you if they have to introduce themselves to you again.'

Rebecca felt a little relieved. She didn't want to give the impression that she was either aloof or uninterested.

'Trust me, you are the most interesting thing to happen round here since they extended the freeway back in the nineties.'

Rebecca looked at him to see if he was joking, but although he was smiling his face said it was the truth.

Rebecca wasn't sure she wanted to be an interesting thing. She had hoped she would just be able to merge into the background, but realised now how foolish that thought had been. Maybe she should have headed to a city instead?

'I mean it. As soon as the bridge was built, the Sheriffs had to go up there to control the crowds.'

Rebecca tried to smother a smile but failed. Will laughed at her expression and then they were back at Rebecca's new front door and she couldn't remember how they had got there.

Will pushed the door open, which Rebecca realised she had failed to lock, and carried the shopping bags to the kitchen counter.

She released Jack from his lead, and he jumped straight back on to the sofa.

'I think I need to get a blanket for Jack to sit on,' she said, wondering if she should make the dog get down. It wasn't as if it were her sofa, after all. Will disappeared into the bedroom and came back with a blanket.

'Mum always keeps this in the cupboard in case people bring their dogs.'

Will cocked his head at Jack who clambered off the sofa, grumbling. Rebecca took one end and Will the other and together they covered the sofa. Jack jumped back on, turned around on the spot a few times to and then sat down.

'Well, he's making himself at home,' Will said as the phone in his pocket beeped.

'He certainly gives that impression. Can I make you some tea?' Rebecca asked.

Will was looking at his phone.

'Sorry — I can't. I've had some emails come into the station that I need to check on.'

Rebecca nodded, unconvinced by the excuse.

'I thought it was your day off?' she added half jokily, not sure why she felt suddenly reluctant for Will to leave.

'I told you, I'm never off duty.'

Rebecca blinked. Why had he sounded so accusatory? It wasn't as if she had begged him for his help — well, not since the creature incident anyway. He was the one who had insisted on using his free time to help her.

She watched as he let himself out, eyes down and fixed on his phone, without so much as a goodbye.

From the sofa, Jack growled as the door slammed.

'I can't figure him out either,' she said to the dog, ruffling his ears. 'It's a good job we don't need him, isn't it, boy?'

Rebecca would never admit it but it had been rather nice to have someone around who seemed to care — but if that turned out to be just an act, well, Rebecca didn't have time for such games.

'I'll put the kettle on, then,' she said to Jack, who yawned widely and went back to dozing.

6

Rebecca had just settled herself on the sofa with a cup of tea in one hand and a copy of the local paper — which she had bought at the grocery store — in the other, when there was a firm knock on the door.

Jack's ears perked up but he made no move to get up and she was fairly sure that even if he did, he hadn't mastered the art of opening doors, so she shuffled herself forward and managed to get to her feet.

It was becoming a real effort to get up from a sitting position and Rebecca could only imagine that would get worse before the baby arrived.

She had a hand on the door when the knocking came again, more impatient this time and Rebecca felt a flare of anger. Whoever it was needed to learn some manners! It wasn't as if she was in a condition to run across the small room at the first sound of knocking.

She took a deep breath. She was new here and she didn't want to ruffle any feathers and so she plastered a smile on her face and opened the door.

Rebecca wasn't all that surprised to see Will Hayes standing on her doorstep — after all, she only really knew two people in the town — but what she was surprised about was the expression on his face. And the fact that he was now in uniform, despite the fact that it was his day off.

'Hello. Did you come back to join me for a cup of tea after all?' Rebecca tried for a little levity but it fell on stony ground. She took a step back.

'Ms Buckingham.' He said her name very carefully. 'I need you to come with me.'

Of all the things she could imagine he was about to say, that was not one of them. He stood on her door step looking every inch the Sheriff going about his duties.

'Excuse me?' Rebecca said, feeling a wave of fear and a little bit of anger. What was going on?

'I have received some information about you and I'm afraid you are going to have to accompany me to the Sheriff's office.'

'What kind of information?' Rebecca asked, her voice shaking. She had known their reach would be long, but to find her here, so quickly — that didn't seem possible.

'It would be better to discuss this matter at the station,' Will said harshly.

Rebecca felt Jack appear at her side. He was leaning into her leg as if he knew she needed some support. Rebecca's mind whirled as her worse fears seemed to be coming true. The world was falling away from her and she couldn't seem to work out which way was up. Her knees were shaking with the strain of maintaining her balance.

Strong hands reached for her as she desperately felt for the door to give her some support. She couldn't faint, not now; she needed to keep herself together, too much was at stake.

'Let me help you,' Will said; his voice had softened a little and Rebecca let herself be led to the sofa. Once she could feel it behind her, she collapsed into it.

Will disappeared from her view and then reappeared with a glass of water. He handed it to her wordlessly.

'I'm sorry,' he said, and he sounded like he meant it.

Rebecca shook her head. She barely knew the man but knew he was simply doing his job. He had no idea what he was getting into, and she knew in that moment she was going to have to try and keep him and the rest of the town out of it.

'I've had a report from London Metropolitan Police that you may have been travelling on a false passport.'

Rebecca coughed on her mouthful of water which made Will lean towards her, as if he felt he needed to do something, but wasn't sure what, in light of her pregnant state.

'I can assure you I'm not,' Rebecca said, wriggling forward so she could stand up.

'Stay where you are for a moment. I don't want you passing out.'

Rebecca relaxed a little.

'My passport is in my bag and I have a folder in my suitcase with all my other personal documents.'

'The report said you may be carrying other false documents.'

Rebecca took a moment to absorb this. She had known that they were powerful people, but to get the police in the UK involved . . . that spoke of a level of reach that she had not considered.

She could feel her ears ringing at the thought. Where could she go? Where could she hide? She had been sure she might be safe here on the other side of the world for a couple of weeks at least, but now she would need to leave, immediately.

Assuming Will would let her.

'I'll get them and you can look at them,' Rebecca said. What she needed to do was prove it was all a mistake and then run, as soon and as fast as she could.

Will held up his hands.

'I can get them, with your permission?'

Rebecca nodded. She had nothing to hide and in truth was still not one hundred percent sure that her legs would support her if she tried to stand. She watched as Will picked up her handbag and pulled out her passport. He looked at it and then placed it on the coffee table.

'Your suitcase?' he asked politely.

'On the bed,' Rebecca said.

Will walked into the bedroom and then returned with the suitcase. He placed it on the coffee table and opened it so that Rebecca was able to see what he was doing. The paper folder was on the top and Will removed it before looking through it. He pulled out Rebecca's birth certificate and compared it with the passport details.

'Look at the date it was issued,' Rebecca said.

Will's eyes scanned the document. 'September fifth, ninety-one.'

'Three days after my birthday. I can assure you they are genuine.'

'Clearly there's been some kind of mistake,' Will said, although he was frowning. 'It's strange they would make such a mistake and then go to all the trouble of contacting me. It must have taken quite a lot of work to track you down.'

Will turned his gaze towards her and his eyes were troubled.

In that moment Rebecca knew she only had one choice. She had to tell him and hope that he would believe what, even to her own ears, seemed like a fantastical story.

'Perhaps the rental car company? They have trackers in all their vehicles.'

Will nodded. 'But why? I mean, why go to all that trouble for a fake pass-port? Usually they hand this sort of thing over to the US authorities to look into.' Will seemed to be processing all this and Rebecca let him think. She didn't really know how to start her story.

'Rebecca, what's going on?' he asked. His words sounded soft to her ears and it sounded as if he wanted to know. Perhaps he cared.

Jack dropped his head on to Rebecca's lap and stared up at her, giving the impression that he wanted her to tell Will, that he trusted Will. Rebecca almost laughed at the idea she was now taking imaginary advice from a dog.

'I don't know where to start and I doubt you would believe me,' she said, shaking her head.

'I want to help.'

Rebecca looked up at him sharply. He seemed genuine but she couldn't draw him into this. Too many people had been hurt already.

'If you want to help then you need to let me leave and soon. I promise I'll go far away and you'll never have to deal with any of this again.'

'I can't do that,' Will said.

'None of what they are saying is true,' Rebecca said feeling desperation replace some of the fear. She had to make him understand.

Will studied her for a few moments.

'Then you need to explain what's going on and then I promise I'll help you.'

'You can't help me — no one can!'

Rebecca's voice was louder than she intended, and Jack whimpered. She brushed the fur on his head. Somehow Jack's presence made things feel a little better, as if she wasn't entirely alone.

'If you're in trouble, I'm sure I can. If you've done something wrong, then . . .'

Rebecca glared at him and he stopped talking.

'The only thing I've done wrong is fall in love with a man who wasn't who he said he was!' She slapped a hand across her mouth as if to physically stop herself from saying any more.

Will seemed to take this on board.

'The baby's father? He's in trouble?'

'He *is* trouble,' Rebecca said miserably. There didn't seem any point holding back now. Will was clearly curious and no doubt would dig until he discovered the truth, or at least the version of the truth that the family had put out there.

'What kind of trouble?'

'Serious trouble — or at least his family is.'

'Organised crime?' Will asked, sounding a little incredulous.

Rebecca sighed; she didn't blame him. If someone had told her the story before it happened to her she probably would have reacted the same.

'I don't know all of it but I know enough to know that they are behind all sorts of criminal activity in the UK.'

Will whistled. 'And it seems like they have some friends in the police, too.'

'I had no idea about that, but nothing would surprise me now.'

'So, you fell in love with a crook?'

'Not exactly. I fell in love with a man who I believed to be just an average guy. What I didn't know was who James's father was, or that James was due to join his father's business.'

'And when you found out?'

'I told him that he had a choice — me and the baby, or his family. I said I couldn't be part of his family.' She turned to Will, desperate for him to understand. 'They were involved in drugs and who knows what else. I can't bring my baby up in that world — I won't.'

Will reached out a hand for her arm and squeezed it. 'I understand,' he said.

Rebecca sniffed as she felt tears start to fall.

'And I take it that he chose his family?'

Rebecca wiped angrily at her tears.

'He said he could never leave, even if he wanted to. He said the family would never let me go either, not as I was carrying his dad's grandchild.'

Will blew air out of his cheeks. 'So you ran.'

'I didn't have a choice.'

'I can see that.'

'You believe me?'

'It's a wild story,' Will said, running a hand through his hair, leaving it standing up in places.

Rebecca closed her eyes. Had she been right to tell him? If he didn't believe her, then who knew what he would do? She could almost feel the looming presence of the Barter family.

'I don't see why you would make up a story like that, or travel all the way here, and it makes more sense of why the UK police have gone to all the trouble of tracking you here.'

'That's why I have to leave — and soon. I won't ask any more of you than keeping that fact quiet for as long as you feel you can.'

'You can't leave.'

Rebecca shifted a little in her seat. Her car was still back at the cabin and it wasn't as if she was in a state to run anywhere — assuming she could outrun him, which she doubted she could, even if she wasn't pregnant.

'Relax, Rebecca. I don't mean you can't leave like that; of course you can. From my perspective you haven't done anything wrong. What I mean is that I'm not sure running will help.'

'Then what do you suggest?'

Rebecca knew she sounded annoyed and she had no right to take things out on him but there was so much at stake. She crossed her arms over her belly as if she could physically protect her child from its father and all the trouble that would surely follow in his wake.

'Stay here. We'll keep you safe.'

Rebecca wanted to laugh out loud but it would have been without humour. She bit back the urge.

'How?'

'I trust every person in this town, even the ones that live on the edge of the law.' Will grinned a little, he clearly had someone in mind. 'No one here will betray you.'

Rebecca wanted to scream at Will. He just didn't get it!

'The Barters are powerful — and

they will come for me.'

'Then they'll be met with resistance.'

Rebecca blinked, wondering if Will was joking.

'You can't be serious?'

'It seems to me that you need a long term solution to your problem,' Will said.

'You think that asking this small town to protect me is the answer?'

'No, that would be a temporary solution. We need to take down the Barter family. Then you and the baby will be safe.'

'How do you propose to do that?'

Rebecca felt completely overwhelmed. It wasn't possible, surely? But Will seemed so certain, so confident, that she felt what she had thought she had lost a long time ago . . . a glimmer of hope.

7

Rebecca stared with her mouth open. She knew it wasn't a good look, but she couldn't help it. What Will had just suggested was at best outrageous and at worst highly dangerous. If she had learned anything about the Barter family over the last few months it was that they always got what they wanted, no matter who got in their way.

'There's no way,' she whispered.

'There's always a way,' Will said calmly.

Rebecca swallowed. A small voice inside her told her that Will was right. It was the only way to be free of the Barter family, for her baby to be safe, but still . . .

'How would we know who to trust? Anyone I speak to might be on their payroll.'

'I know someone,' Will said thoughtfully.

'And you trust them not to be involved, not to be in the pockets of these people?'

Rebecca didn't mean to sound incredulous but if the last few weeks had taught her anything it was that the Barters' reach was long.

'With my life,' Will said softly, and he sounded as if he was remembering something.

Rebecca studied his face trying to pick up on some hint as to why he would feel so strongly about that person, something that could reassure her, but Will was giving nothing away.

'I'm not sure, Will,' she said as she struggled off of the sofa to her feet. 'I still think running is my best option, and I can't drag you into this. I don't think you really understand what these people are capable of.'

Will's expression hardened. 'My time in the Army has ensured that nothing could surprise me on that front.' He stood up too. 'It also taught me that some things are worth fighting for.'

'Why do you want to fight for me? You hardly know me — '

The words were falling out of her mouth and she had to force herself to stop. She was so vulnerable right now and the idea that someone was willing to step up and protect her was a powerful feeling — one that might just override her common sense and judgment.

'Because you've done nothing wrong, Rebecca. You and your baby are innocent, and I took an oath to protect innocent people from harm.'

Rebecca studied him. Once again, his face gave nothing away but she felt sure there was more to it. He could protect her by handing her over to the authorities, then his job would be done. He could discharge his duty that way, couldn't he? But he seemed strangely reluctant to do so. The idea was both a comfort and a worry; Rebecca liked to fully understand people's motives.

'Perhaps I should go to the FBI?' It wasn't possible that the Barter family had connections as far as the Bureau, surely?

'Their focus is on activities in this country. Unless you have information about the Barters working here? I suspect they would just direct you to the British authorities.'

Rebecca shook her head.

'Relax, I don't think that's a good idea either. Hence my suggestion that you stay here.'

'I just don't think I can ask you to do that. It's going to bring all sorts of trouble down on you.'

'If it does, and if I think we need to leave, then we can leave.'

'We?' Rebecca asked.

'You don't think I would let you go on the run by yourself? No offence, Rebecca, but I don't think you'd last a day.'

Will was smiling but Rebecca knew she had a face like thunder and his smile turned to a challenging raised eyebrow.

'It wasn't meant as an insult,' he said,

holding his hands out as if he felt the need to placate her. 'This is a foreign country and it's not like you've had any training.'

'And you have?'

Rebecca had a hand on each hip, although she knew the impact was lost a little with her baby bump. It was hard to look completely in control when you were seven months pregnant. People said you glowed, but in reality you just looked a little soft and it tended to engender the desire in people to look after you.

'I *was* in the Army,' he said as if that explained everything.

'And I suppose they focused a lot on escaping from a British crime family, did they?'

Rebecca wasn't sure why they were arguing. He had offered to help her and in the current circumstances she really could use the help, but somehow, she felt the need to stamp on some of the 'helpless pregnant lady' talk.

'I was a Ranger. Our missions were

covert and involved infiltrating enemy territories undetected. I think I'm as qualified as you're going to get.'

Rebecca opened her mouth, but no words came. There wasn't much she could say in relation to that. He was right, he did seem reasonably qualified for the job — but she still couldn't understand why he would be so willing to lay his whole life on the line for a stranger he had just met.

'I will shoulder more than my share of the task, whatever it may be, one hundred percent and then some.'

Rebecca didn't know what to say, so she kept quiet. Will seemed to be lost to a memory.

'Part of the Ranger Creed,' he said when he returned from wherever he had been.

'It's part of who I am,' he added.

There were still missing pieces in the mystery that was Will, but perhaps it was starting to make sense. They stood together, in the small room that functioned as her kitchen and lounge, and looked at each other.

'So, if I'm staying here . . . ' Rebecca wasn't quite ready to concede that she was definitely staying, although she knew in truth that she was. 'What do we need to do?'

'You'll need to move in here permanently,' Will said and he looked as if he was bracing himself for Rebecca to argue, but she didn't. Now that she knew the Barter family had found her, the cabin was the last place she wanted to be.

'OK.'

Will looked surprised, but only briefly before he carried on. 'I'm going to head up to the cabin to do some work.'

'Fix the door?' Rebecca asked. It seemed a little pointless since no one would be staying there, and she couldn't really see her renting it out to poor unsuspecting visitors when she knew the Barter family might already be aware that she owned it.

'And some,' Will said turning to her

with a grin. 'I'm going to set a little trap for whoever they decide to send.'

Will's eyes were flashing and Rebecca had the impression that he was enjoying concocting the plan he was coming up with. But for herself, she felt a stab of worry. Will was sticking his head in the lion's mouth and she wasn't sure how she felt about that. Being a Ranger and fighting for your country was one thing, but doing the same for a complete stranger seemed something else.

'You need to be careful — don't underestimate them,' Rebecca said, not bothering to keep the warning tone from her voice.

'Never underestimate your enemy, Rebecca,' Will said — and that look was back.

'And don't do anything illegal,' Rebecca added. Will's zeal was starting to concern her.

'Don't worry, I'll stay the right side of the law. I'm not planning on hurting anyone — just sending out a clear warning.'

'A warning?'

'A warning to stay away. A warning that this town, and all the people in it, are protected.'

With that Will was gone.

★ ★ ★

There was a knock at the door. Jack's ears pricked up but he didn't bark or growl so Rebecca took that as a good sign.

She went to the door. Will had said he would return later with some deadbolts and window locks to make her new home more secure. Rebecca knew she should be grateful, but the desire to run was still strong inside her. The idea of more locks on the door made her feel trapped, not safer, but she had not said any of this to Will. It didn't seem fair, considering the lengths he was going to in order to keep her safe.

'Who is it?' she asked through the closed door, just as Will had told her to.

'It's Peggy, sweetheart. I've brought

you over some lunch.'

Rebecca pulled open the door and Peggy's smiling but concerned face almost made her cry.

'Oh, my darlin',' she said, placing the plate of food on the small table and pulling Rebecca into her arms. Rebecca wasn't used to be hugged by strangers — but Peggy suddenly felt like family.

'I knew something must be up. I'm mighty glad you decided to stay here, where you'll be safe.'

Rebecca didn't ask if Will had told Peggy everything. She didn't need to and she was glad he had. She didn't think she could face going through it all again. Somehow saying it out loud made it feel more real, and the danger even closer than it probably was.

When Rebecca had stopped shaking, Peggy took her hand and led her to the table. Rebecca dutifully took her seat as Peggy took the lid off the plate of food.

'I brought you salad and roast chicken. You need to be getting those vitamins,' Peggy said as she bustled into the kitchen and put the kettle on. 'And I brought you some herbal teabags too, honey.'

'You're so kind,' Rebecca said, feeling the emotion build up once more. 'You hardly know me and yet ... ' She couldn't finish the words out loud, the consequences of Will and his family protecting her were too awful to think about.

'Nonsense. If this town is anything, it looks after the people that need its help and if I may say so, you would be one of those people, and so would your baby.'

Peggy brought two mugs of tea over and took a seat at the table.

'Now, I've made you an appointment with the local doctor. After everything you've been through I thought it would be good for you to get a thorough check-up,' Peggy said, in a voice that would not brook an argument.

'That's very kind of you,' Rebecca said as her mind went to her small amount of savings that she had been able to bring with her. Healthcare in

America was all private and so no doubt it would cost her more than she imagined.

'And you can stop looking so worried. Our doctor has reasonable rates,' Peggy added. 'Now, how are you for money? I don't mean to pry and all — only to help,' she added, even though she seemed totally unfazed at asking such a personal question.

'I have some . . . ' Rebecca said cautiously.

'Well, I don't imagine you had much time to prepare for your trip. We can probably get that cabin of yours rented out again, so that'll bring you in a little extra cash.'

Peggy looked lost in thought.

'What I need is a job,' Rebecca said out loud.

'No. What you need is to rest in your condition and not be worrying about things like money,' Peggy said, her voice stern.

'I need to pay my way,' Rebecca said equally forcefully and the two women locked gazes, before Peggy nodded, seemingly accepting Rebecca's need to do something herself about her own situation.

'I'll see what I can come up with, then. What did you do before you had to leave home?'

'I was a translator. I speak French and Italian. I was hoping that perhaps some of the local high school students might need some extra tuition, but I'm not sure whether they even study languages.'

When Peggy looked at Rebecca, her eyes were triumphant.

'I'm sure I can round up some folks up who would be interested in learning.'

Rebecca smiled. Somehow, she had no doubt that Peggy would do just that — whether the individuals had an interested in learning a new language or not.

'And that will be something you can do while taking the weight off. It shouldn't be too strenuous on you or the baby.'

Peggy seemed to fully approve of the idea and Rebecca wouldn't be surprised if she had her first student by the end of the day.

8

Peggy was true to her word and before the day was out she had rounded up three people who said they had a desire to learn either French or Italian, and her first lesson was booked in for later that week.

Rebecca couldn't imagine what favours Peggy had to call in, but she was grateful. If was certainly more than she had hoped for when she arrived in the country. At least she would be able to pay for the basics like food, and make a contribution towards her rent.

Peggy had invited her to have her evening meal over in the diner and Rebecca, still feeling somewhat overwhelmed by the events of the day, had readily agreed. She was just putting some food down for Jack, who seemed to be able to consume a whole bowl of dog food in a single mouthful, when there was a knock at the door.

Despite the reassurances of both Peggy and Will, her nerves seemed to all switch on at once. Will had returned and fixed an extra bolt and a chain to the door but still, Rebecca didn't want to answer it. What if they had found her? After all, they now knew what town she was living in!

Will had reported back to the British authorities that all of Rebecca's documents were genuine — Rebecca knew he'd had to. If he hadn't, he'd said, they might have considered pressing the authorities in the US to take action themselves and Will would not be able to shield her from that. No, it had been better to tell them all was in order — but that would also, no doubt, send the message to the Barter family.

The knock sounded again, but this time there was also a muffled voice from the other side of the door.

'Rebecca, it's Will.'

She felt both relieved and a little foolish.

'Sorry,' she called through the door as she undid the bolts and pulled it open. 'I was just feeding Jack.'

Will looked from Rebecca to Jack, who was now sat by his empty food bowl and whining as if he was waiting to be fed.

Rebecca followed Will's gaze and rolled her eyes. 'That won't work, Jack. You've been fed.'

Will laughed, and it was a warm and reassuring sound. Rebecca smiled at him.

'Dinner in nought to five seconds, huh?' Will said leaning down to stroke Jack's head as he wandered over.

'Something like that,' Rebecca said.

'Ma said you'd accepted her invite, so I thought I could come and escort you.'

Rebecca smiled. She figured she was probably safe to cover the ten steps between her front door and the back door of the diner, but it was nice of him to offer.

Will opened the door and together

they crossed the yard.

'I should warn you that Ma has a bit of a surprise for you,' Will said, as Rebecca pushed the back door into the diner.

'Rebecca!' Peggy greeted her with a tight hug. 'I've invited a few folks from town to have dinner and I also asked around to see if anyone had any baby things they no longer needed.'

Rebecca couldn't speak. The diner was nearly full — and not just with people. Two tables had been pushed together and were laden down with every type of baby paraphernalia she could ever have wished for. There was a stroller, a car seat, piles of neatly folded baby clothes, and what looked like the frame of a cot.

Rebecca stared as her voice caught in her throat. She wanted to say thank you but that seemed so inadequate and in truth she didn't think she could speak.

'I don't know what to say,' she finally managed to force out. She turned to face the beaming crowd with tears in her eyes. 'You've been so generous, and you don't even know me.' Rebecca's voice wobbled, and she knew she was on the verge of breaking down in messy sobs.

'You don't need to say anything,' Peggy said kindly. 'I just mentioned to a few folks that you'd just arrived and hadn't had much chance to get things in for the baby. Word travels fast round these parts and before I knew it, folks were turning up at my door with things they no longer had a use for.'

Peggy pulled her back into a hug, which gave Rebecca a few moments to compose herself.

'Thank you,' Rebecca said to the crowd, who all smiled back and burst into applause.

'Right, enough of that — now we eat,' Peggy said, directing Rebecca to one of the few empty seats. Will slipped into the booth beside her.

Opposite were a young couple.

'This is Tina, my youngest sister, and her boyfriend, Paul,' Will said.

'Hi,' Rebecca said feeling, a little shy.

Tina looked as if she was in her late teens and Paul about the same age.

'They're headed back to college next week but they were keen to meet you before they left.'

Rebecca raised an eyebrow at this, she couldn't believe that anyone would be that keen to meet her — unless they knew her circumstances. Surely Will hadn't told them?

'Don't worry, Rebecca. New people always create a stir of interest. Most of the town have lived here for generations and newcomers are like shiny new toys,' Tina said, smiling.

Rebecca felt instantly that she liked the girl, seeing a younger Peggy sitting before her.

'Of course, Will used to be the star of the show,' Tina said teasingly. 'What with all his top secret foreign travel.' Tina leaned across the table and pretended to whisper conspiratorially, 'He would never tell us where he'd been or what he'd been up to.'

Tina glanced at her brother and laughed as Will shifted a little in his seat.

Rebecca smiled; it seemed that Peggy wasn't the only woman in Will's life who could take him to task. It made such a contrast to Will in work mode and Rebecca had to admit she quite liked this other side of him.

She also had the impression that Will hadn't told Tina about her situation after all, and that was a relief. The fewer people knew, the better.

Looking around at the generosity of the town, Rebecca felt a flash of guilt that she was putting them all in harm's way. Will must have seen the look on her face as she felt him reach a hand out for hers under the table. It was the briefest touch, and later Rebecca would wonder if she had imagined it or willed it to happen, but in that moment it was enough to reassure her that she wasn't alone in this — and that, somehow, Will would keep the town safe as well.

Rebecca smiled up at him gratefully

and he held her gaze for a second before she tore her gaze away, conscious that she couldn't allow whatever was happening to happen.

When she looked back at the other guests she could see that Tina was looking at them both, curiosity written across her face. Rebecca knew that she would need to be more guarded. Will deserved to be happy, not to be entangled in her situation. He had already been so kind, and she needed to return the favour and keep any thoughts of her feelings for him strictly to herself.

* * *

After dinner, Will and Paul carried all the gifts from the diner to Rebecca's home, which felt as if it was getting smaller every time they brought something new in. She knew, from reading books and from friends, that babies needed a lot of stuff, but still. She had no idea where she was going to put it all!

'I'll leave the crib disassembled for

now,' Will said. 'Give you a bit more space until you need it.' He flicked a gaze at Rebecca's stomach.

'I still have a few months to go,' Rebecca said noting the look without the accompanying question.

Will nodded as if he were filing this information away for later and then looked at his watch. 'I'm going to head out. I want to do one last check of the cabin.'

Rebecca nodded. Will's plan still filled her with unease, but it was clear that this type of situation was more within his skill set than hers.

'Don't look so worried. It's just a message.'

'But then what?'

Rebecca hadn't meant to ask the question but somehow it had slipped out.

'They get the message that you're protected.'

'And what makes you think they won't just come back with greater numbers?'

'It would be a risk. I imagine they thought they could nab you from the cabin, make it look like you decided to leave and that no one would think anything of it.'

Rebecca knew she couldn't go back, that she couldn't raise her baby in that environment, but she also knew that she couldn't bear the thought of putting these people who had been so kind to her at risk.

'I'm not sure . . . maybe I should just take my chances and leave. It's a big country and I'm sure I can disappear.'

'Perhaps if you were on you own, but with a baby? I really do think you should stay here.'

He looked at her as if he were trying to work out what she might do.

'You'll be safe here, I promise,' he said and walked towards the door.

Rebecca watched him go, knowing she had made up her mind. She couldn't put them at risk.

I wasn't right or fair to drag them all into this.

Will might understand the risks that the Barter family presented, but she was sure the rest of the town didn't.

Will pulled the door open.

'Promise me you'll stay here till I get back? I'm going to stake out the cabin and see if we have any unfriendly visitors overnight.'

Rebecca steeled herself to lie. It was not her strong point and many people had told her that her face gave away her every thought and feeling. Could she stand there and lie to this man's face, even if it was for his own good?

'I promise,' Rebecca said, surprised at the steadiness in her voice. She felt as if the last few weeks had changed her in ways she had not been able to imagine — and one of the ways, it seemed, was her ability to tell a lie.

Will studied her for a few moments and then nodded before pulling the door closed behind him. 'Make sure you put the bolts across. Call me if you need anything,' Will's voice sounded through the door.

'Thank you,' Rebecca said.

It didn't seem enough for all that he had done and for what he was offering to do.

She listened as his footsteps sounded across the courtyard and then the back door to the diner opened and closed.

Rebecca allowed herself one moment to take a deep breath.

She would write Peggy and Will a note, explaining why she had to leave and to thank them for everything. Maybe she would even add that she might try to come back one day, to thank them properly, although she couldn't ever imagine a time when that might be possible.

She needed to get lost. She needed to become someone else, someone the Barters couldn't find. But first she needed to get away.

She walked into the bedroom and picked up her suitcase, putting it on the bed. Fighting against her warring emotions, she pushed only what she absolutely needed into her carry-on case. She would need to travel light.

Jack appeared beside her and whined.

'I'm not sure if you're allowed to travel on the bus,' Rebecca said. 'And I don't know any other way to get away.'

Jack whined some more and the guilt Rebecca was already feeling doubled.

'It's not that I don't want to take you with me, boy, but I need to find somewhere to stay and that will be harder with a dog. You understand, don't you? I'll ask Will to look after you, I promise.'

When Rebecca had written her note — after several failed attempts — and picked up her bag and walked to the door, Jack followed her like a shadow.

'Please don't make this any harder than it already is. If I could think of any way to take you with me, I would.'

Rebecca pleaded with the dog but he just looked up at her with sad eyes and she felt her heart contract. It was bad enough walking away from Peggy and the rest of the town, after everything they had done for her, but could she really leave Jack behind to a fate that was not certain?

She shook her head sadly, crossed the room and picked up the lead that Will had bought for Jack. She leaned down and clipped it onto the dog's collar and together they headed out into the night . . .

9

Rebecca held up the map she had found in the lounge with the various other tourist information leaflets. The bus station was down the far end of Main Street.

Main Street was nearly deserted, and Rebecca already had her story ready in case she bumped into anyone . . . she was just taking Jack for his last walk of the day before bed. She would just have to hope they wouldn't ask why she was carrying a bag that made her look ready for travel.

The bus station didn't really live up to expectations. There was no station. Tickets were advertised in the nearby dry cleaners which thankfully was still open.

Rebecca tied Jack to a lamp post, told him firmly to wait, and went inside. The last bus of the day would take her to

Charlotte, where she would find some-where to stay. Then they would head off — to where she hadn't figured out. Or maybe she would get on a train? She was sure the trains would run later than the local buses and then she could really disappear — assuming that dogs were allowed on trains.

An elderly woman sat behind the counter, lost in her book of crosswords. She looked up as Rebecca walked in and the surprise registered on her face. It seemed unlikely that she didn't know who Rebecca was.

'Good evening,' Rebecca said. 'I was wondering if I could buy an open ticket to Charlotte? I think I'd like to go up there for the day at some point this week.'

Rebecca had researched her story to make sure it would work, but she still felt bad. The need to lie was real but that didn't mean it sat comfortably with her.

'That I'll be nine dollars,' the woman said staring at her with open curiosity.

'Thank you. I hear it's a lovely town.'

The older woman sniffed. 'I prefer my own town, but I'm told it's quite popular with tourists.'

Rebecca was a little taken aback by the attitude. This was the first person she had met who hadn't been openly warm and friendly, and if she was honest it was a little refreshing.

'I expect I'll feel the same. I do love it here.'

That was the truth but Rebecca could still feel her cheeks burn. She did love it here but that didn't mean she was going to stay. She wanted to, quite desperately, but she knew she couldn't. The woman nodded but said nothing.

'Well, I best be getting back to my dog. He's expecting a walk.'

'Go careful, mind,' the woman said and Rebecca smiled before hurrying out of the door.

Jack was waiting for her and leaned up to lick her hand. Rebecca smiled at him. It was probably foolish to take him with her. It would no doubt make things more difficult, but at the same time, it was nice to have a friendly face with her. He might just be a dog to some people but he made her feel less alone.

Rebecca untied him and walked him further down the road so they would be out of the immediate view of the Dry Cleaners, but so that she could still see the bus stop.

'Right,' Rebecca said to Jack. 'You can travel on the bus if you fit into a bag.' Rebecca looked from the bag she had brought to the rather large dog. 'It's not going to be the most comfortable ride but I'm hoping that once we get on and settled I can let you out.'

Jack leaned against her and Rebecca took that as a sign he understood.

The bag was a large shopper with a flat bottom and it didn't close, so even if Jack was forced to sit in it, his head would be free.

Jack jumped in. It was a tight squeeze, but he seemed happy to try and make it work. She scratched him behind the ears. They didn't have to wait too long, as the silver bus pulled up at the kerb and the doors at the front opened. The driver looked out — a woman in her thirties — and took in the dog in the bag. For a moment Rebecca was worried she would refuse to let them on.

'Well, that's a mighty tight squeeze for such a big fella.'

'He'll behave, I promise,' Rebecca said.

She couldn't leave Jack tied to a lamp post — and this was the last bus so she had no time to take him back to Peggy's.

'I'm sure he will, but why don't you get him out of that bag? As long as he sits on the floor, I'm sure the other folks won't mind.'

Jack seemed to have understood every word as he jumped out of the bag and climbed up the bus steps, before sitting down and waiting for Rebecca.

She smiled gratefully at the driver, showed her ticket and then she and Jack found a seat, near to the front. The driver closed the doors and the bus headed off.

Rebecca stared out of the window, trying to fix the sights of the town in her memory. Jack sat on the floor and rested his head in her lap and Rebecca stroked his ears, more for her own comfort than his.

The bus quickly left the town limits and made its way up a narrow road that wound its way up into the mountains. The turns were tight, but the driver seemed completely unfazed. Rebecca felt her stomach lurch every time the bus seemed to near the edge and after a few turns decided that she should close her eyes.

The journey to Charlotte was a couple of hours according to the timetable, and she should probably rest while she could.

Resting was easier said than done, Rebecca thought. She was exhausted and would have loved nothing more than to curl up on a comfy bed with Jack at her side and sleep, but she couldn't. Not when she knew that the Barter family had found her.

She would need to find somewhere she could disappear and a larger city seemed her best bet.

'What on earth?' The bus driver said out loud.

Rebecca's attention was caught immediately and she opened her eyes.

'What is it?' Rebecca asked, not wanting to know the answer.

'Blue flashing lights. I slowed down to let them pass but they seem to want me to stop . . . '

Rebecca swivelled in her seat and saw the blue flashes. Surely Will couldn't have discovered she had left and where she was headed so quickly?

Then another thought struck her. What if it wasn't Will? What if it was some other person working under the guise of law enforcement but really in league with the Barter Family?

Rebecca felt a wave of nausea that had nothing to do with the tight bends on the road.

'Sorry folks, looks like we're going to be delayed,' the driver said, looking apologetically in the large rear-view mirror.

Rebecca wanted to beg her to keep driving but she knew it was pointless. There was no way to explain her fears without sounding like a crazy person and even if she could convince the driver to keep driving, whoever was following would simply stay on their tail until they reached Charlotte.

The bus came to a controlled halt and the driver opened the doors at the front.

'Good evening officer. What can I do for you?' The driver smiled pleasantly as the man climbed aboard the bus.

Rebecca felt Will's presence before she could see him. At first there was overwhelming relief that it was him — but that was quickly replaced with dread. Will would insist she went back to town and that would be bad for everyone. She had to make him understand that this was the only way.

'Miss Buckingham. There has been an emergency and I was sent to find you,' Will said the words slowly and Rebecca got the impression they were for the driver and passengers' benefit.

'What kind of emergency?'

Rebecca knew she was stalling but also that the people on the bus would be curious and it seemed like a good excuse to delay the inevitable telling off that was coming her way.

'The doctor has some results back from your recent check-up. He says there's no need for concern, but you need to come back to the clinic as soon as possible to be treated.'

Rebecca's hand went to her belly in response even though she knew it wasn't true. The doctor had said everything was fine. 'I was on my way to Charlotte. I can see a doctor there.' Rebecca hoped that Will was getting the message.

'The doctor was insistent,' Will said, holding out a hand.

'You should do as he says, dear,' an older woman behind her said. 'I don't mean to pry but that little one is a precious gift. I'm sure you can go to Charlotte when you're both feeling better.'

Rebecca smiled, knowing the woman was just being kind but also knowing that she had no choice now. If she didn't get off the bus she was going to look like the worst kind of mother-to-be.

'Of course, you're right,' she said and struggled to her feet. 'Thank you,' she said to Will, feeling anything but thankful.

He held out his hand, took her bag from her as well as Jack's lead, and led the way off the bus.

'Sorry for all the trouble, ma'am,' Will said ducking his head to the driver.

'No problem, officer.' The driver smiled. 'You look after yourself, Miss,' she said to Rebecca.

'Thank you,' Rebecca said as she navigated her way down the steps.

Will had already dumped her bag in the back of his Sheriff's car and was loading Jack into the back seat.

'Get in,' Will said, his words clipped and dripping with disapproval.

Rebecca felt a flash of anger. He had a right to be put out, but to treat her as if she had committed a crime was a step too far. She hadn't followed his advice but that was her right — and he needed to stop treating her as if she had broken the law.

She opened her mouth to speak.

'Now!' he shouted, and she was so shocked by his reaction that she climbed into the passenger seat. What else was she going to do — stand on the side of a narrow country road in the dark?

Rebecca angled herself into the car, not easy and certainly not quick, and before she had barely clicked her seatbelt in place, Will, had put his foot to the floor. The car leapt forward, skidding on the gravel that formed the small layby.

Rebecca knew he was angry with her but this was a bit much. She was pregnant after all, or had he forgotten?

Driving like the devil himself was on their heels!

'I know you must be angry with me but . . . ' Rebecca started to say.

Will flicked a look in her direction and then turned back to focus on the road. The expression didn't show anger but something else. What was it? Rebecca couldn't be sure but her body seemed to respond and a shiver ran down her spine.

She reached out a hand for the dashboard as Will took a corner at high speed. The back wheels started to lose their grip and Rebecca was sure the car would roll, that Will would lose control, but he seemed to tap the brakes and the fishtailing stopped and the wheels found purchase.

As soon as they were on a steady path again, Will floored the accelerator.

Rebecca was forced back in to her seat and she let out a squeak, her arms forming a protective circle around the baby inside her.

She felt rather than saw Will glance at

her. For her part her eyes were fixed upon the road; if disaster was coming she wanted to see it. The car seemed to slow, almost imperceptibly but there it was. Rebecca dragged her eyes from the winding road and looked at Will.

'Sorry,' Will said, his eyes fixed ahead. 'We need distance.'

'Distance from what?' Rebecca said the words out loud, but her brain had already connected the dots. Something had sent Will after her, and not just the desire for her to stay in the town. Something worse, something that had frightened even him.

The fear wasn't new to Rebecca; she felt as if she had been living with it for years when in fact it had really only been weeks.

She knew what the Barter family were capable of but perhaps Will's eyes had finally been opened to the reality. The reality that if she had stayed, she would have put so many people at risk. Maybe now he understood? Maybe he was going to take her away from the town and then let her go free?

Rebecca frowned. If he wanted to put some distance between her and the town, then why hadn't he simply let her go on the bus? It didn't make sense, unless his excuse was genuine. Perhaps there was something wrong with her, or with the baby? Perhaps the doctor did need to see her urgently.

'If something is wrong with me or the baby, you have to tell me.' Rebecca's voice was high pitched and filled with fear.

Will looked at her sharply. 'The doctor says you're both fine,' he said as if he wasn't sure why she was asking the question.

'But you said . . . '

'I said that to give a reason for chasing down the bus and making you get off. Ideally we would have disappeared quietly but that wasn't possible.'

'Wait . . . we?' Rebecca's brain seemed to have focused in on the word like a laser.

'I told you. I'm not going to let you go on the run on your own. It's not safe,' he snapped.

Rebecca shook her head. This was exactly what she was trying to avoid. Having someone by her side was a huge comfort — particularly someone like Will — but she also knew it was selfish. She had got herself into this situation and she alone was responsible for it. She couldn't drag him in to it. She had no idea what lay ahead but it wasn't fair to him.

'You should have let me go,' Rebecca said. 'I'm not your responsibility.'

'And I told you that's not how we do things where I'm from.'

'For how long?' Rebecca asked and twisted in her seat so that she could see his reaction. 'I may have to run for years. You can't possibly stay with me for that long! You have a life, and people who need you.'

She wanted him to understand, she needed him to, but deep down she knew that if he didn't leave soon she would lose the ability to ask him to go. She told herself it was because she felt safe with him, that she felt less alone, but it was far more than that. And she had no right, no right at all, to do anything but push those feelings down deep and to run and to try and forget about all him.

'I have a plan, Rebecca. I told you. You can't run forever either. We need to end this.'

'There is no 'we',' Rebecca said.

She knew she should push him away, be rude and hurtful, but she didn't think she had the strength to.

'Look, you can drive me to the train station and see me safely on a train. Then you will have done your duty.'

'I told you,' Will said and his voice sounded stubborn. 'I have a plan. Once this is over, I promise I'll leave you to get on with your life without me.'

Rebecca stared at him. Will's eyes were fixed on the road and his face displayed no emotion but his hands, gripped so tightly on the steering wheel, gave away his secret. He was hurt that she had tried to run. Hurt that she hadn't trusted him or followed his plan?

She wasn't sure.

A small part of her wanted to believe there was more to it, but she pushed it away. They barely knew each other, and Will was clearly the kind of man who held honour and duty with the highest regard. He was the kind of man who would go out of his way to help a stranger.

You need to remember that, she told herself firmly, *and stop imagining what your deluded heart wants to see.*

'What happened at the cabin?'

She didn't really want to know. Her mind had done enough imagining by itself, but it seemed somehow to be a safe question, ridiculous as that might sound.

'The trap worked. It sent the right message.'

Rebecca took a moment to think about that. If that was true, why wasn't Will simply taking her back to town?

'Then why aren't we heading . . . ?'

She wanted to say home. She had barely been there two days, but it had started to feel like home, started to feel like a place where she could bring up her baby. But she couldn't, she couldn't afford to think about it like that. The thought brought a fresh wave of pain and there was too much pain and loss in her life already.

'Why aren't we heading back to town?' she managed to squeeze the words out of her throat which seemed to have constricted inside her.

'I had a feeling you were making a run for it.'

That wasn't exactly an answer.

'And you tracked me down, but that doesn't explain the direction we're going in.'

Rebecca gestured to the winding road ahead of them. Will's head lights cut a line into the gloom. Will shrugged.

'I had time to think about it all at the cabin and I thought you might be right.'

Rebecca stared at him, knowing the power of silence. If you said nothing, most people felt the need to fill in the gap with more words and often said things they had not intended to.

Unfortunately, Will did not appear to be one of those people. He simply nodded and concentrated on his driving.

There had to be more to it, Rebecca was sure there was. But she was also sure that Will had no intention of sharing anything further with her.

'Are we heading to Charlotte?'

'We're going to make it look like we are.'

The cryptic stuff was starting to get on Rebecca's nerves.

This was her life, after all. It wasn't that she wasn't grateful to Will for all he had done but what she didn't need right now was another person taking over her life and making decisions for her. That was what she was trying to escape from. She had made the mistake of relying on a person — a person she thought she could trust with her life — and she had been wrong.

She wasn't about to make that mistake again.

No, this wasn't just about escaping from her past, from the Barter family — this was about her starting completely afresh, her and her baby.

'Stop the car,' Rebecca said firmly.

Will ignored her.

'Stop the car!' she said more forcefully.

'I can't. We need to keep moving.'

'Stop the car or I will vomit all over it!'

Rebecca injected a certain amount of panic into her voice — not hard under the circumstances. To add to the effect she gripped her belly and leaned forward, pretending to take deep breaths.

She felt Will's eyes look at her and within moments he had pulled the car onto the side of the road. Rebecca pushed open the door and managed to get both feet on the ground before Will was at her side and helping her up.

'These roads can make folks feel sick,' Will said sympathetically. 'And I suppose your condition doesn't help that. I'm sorry.'

Rebecca wasn't sure if he was sorry she was pregnant or sorry his driving had made her feel sick. Neither was important, since she wasn't actually feeling sick at all. She straightened up and Will's expression said it all as he realised he had been played.

'Well?' he said, his arms folded across his chest, one eyebrow raised.

Rebecca felt as if she had been called to the principal's office to explain her reasons for smoking in the bike sheds and that it didn't matter what she said, because no excuse would be good enough.

'I want to know what the plan is. I need to know,' Rebecca said, mirroring his body language, although she couldn't help that something was lost in the fact that it was getting harder to cross her arms over her pregnant stomach.

'You think having this conversation in the pitch dark in the middle of the forest is a good idea?'

He had a point, but Rebecca wasn't about to be put off. 'I'd have been quite happy to have the conversation in the car, but you didn't seem willing to share.'

Will sighed and ran a hand through his hair. He stared at the ground and Rebecca was sure he was counting to ten under his breath. She was starting to feel a little embarrassed that she was causing him so much trouble but quickly pushed it away. It wasn't as if she had asked him to come, and now he seemed to have his heart set on keeping her in the dark. She had promised herself and her unborn child that she was never going to let that happen again.

He looked up and fixed his gaze on her. She didn't look away, as she expected he had intended.

'We're going to a buddy of mine. He lives off-grid so you should be safe there.'

'And you couldn't tell me that because?'

'I wasn't sure you would be happy with the whole off-grid thing,' he said blowing out a breath.

Rebecca frowned. What part of

running for her life didn't he understand?

There was more to it, but it would have to wait. She would never admit it to Will but standing on the side of the road was starting to feel unsafe and all she wanted to do was get back in the car and keep moving.

'Off-grid sounds good but when we get there, I expect you to tell me everything.'

Will walked back to the car. Rebecca stayed where she was. 'I promise. Now please, we need to get back on the road,' he said.

Rebecca climbed back into the car.

Something had happened at the cabin, something that had convinced Will that she needed to run rather than stay. And Will was going to tell her what it was, whether he liked it or not.

10

Rebecca woke with a jolt. The dream she had been having disappeared like water through a cupped hand. She couldn't remember what it had been about, the images fading, but the sensations remained. She was afraid, felt her heart pounding in her chest.

She looked about her.

Will was focused on the road and seemed alert but untroubled. The road was wider now and there was more traffic, two lanes heading in each direction. She felt like they could disappear, except for the fact that they were driving in a marked Sheriff's car, complete with blue lights on the roof that could flash if required. That would be enough to draw attention, but now she was fairly sure they had travelled outside Will's jurisdiction, which was bound to draw notice.

There were no signs of danger around her, or at least no obvious signs, so she put the sensation down to the dream, which now seemed to have completely slipped from her grasp.

'You OK?' Will's voice cut through her thoughts and she jumped a little, even though she knew he was there.

'I must have fallen asleep,' she said, stating what she knew was obvious.

Rebecca looked as a sign appeared ahead of them but they passed it too quickly for her to take in where they were. Not that the names of the towns and cities would make much sense to her.

'You've been out for four hours or so.'

Rebecca's eyes went wide. Four hours? She had slept for four hours and now had absolutely no idea where they were! She wriggled in her seat, feeling stiff. She would give anything to stretch out her legs, not to mention her back.

'We're going to stop soon. Can you hang on for another half an hour?'

Will saying the words out loud seemed to waken her sleeping bladder, which told her, in no uncertain terms, that she needed to pee.

'I'll be fine,' she said ignoring the indignant messages her body was sending her.

Rebecca didn't want to stop until they had to, and it sounded as if Will had somewhere in mind, somewhere that was likely to be safe — or at least as safe as anywhere else they might choose.

'We need to swap vehicles. This one is too easy to track and spot.'

Rebecca nodded.

'I know someone who'll lend me a truck, no questions asked, and we can pick up some supplies before we hit the road. I don't think we should stop to rest often.'

He looked at her and once more his eyes tracked down her to her pregnant belly.

'Fine by me. Keeping moving seems to be a good plan.'

'Just holler if you need me to stop, and I will.'

Rebecca nodded again as her mind returned to the overwhelming conundrum.

'Do you think they're following us?'

'I'm not sure they'll have connected you to me yet, but I don't suppose it'll take long. The locals won't share anything,' he added as if Rebecca might be worried about that.

'I don't want anyone to get hurt,' Rebecca said quickly as her mind replayed the many people who had shown her kindness in her short stay.

'I doubt they'll want to draw that kind of attention, not just yet anyway. Besides, folks in the town can look after themselves.'

Rebecca wanted to feel relieved but all she felt was intense guilt. She had brought trouble on the town that had done nothing but try to help her and they didn't deserve it.

She must have looked stricken because she felt Will reach for her hand and give it a squeeze.

'They'll be fine, I promise. They aren't going to want to create a scene or draw attention to themselves by messing with the town. But right now, we need to focus on putting distance between us.'

Will's hand seemed to linger longer than was necessary for reassurance, and once again Rebecca felt her mind burst forth with all kinds of possible explanations.

The hope was almost painful. Gritting her teeth, she gently moved her hand away and Will returned his to the steering wheel without comment.

Rebecca couldn't bring herself to look at him, afraid of what she might see there. Instead she looked out of the window at the countryside speeding by. There were so many other things that she should be thinking about before some fairytale idea of an impossible romance.

Her baby moved, and she placed a hand gently over the spot. Whether the baby was agreeing with her or not, she wasn't sure.

Will took a side road and headed into a town. It was bigger than Blowing Rock and seemed to be more industrial, judging by the factories that lined the outskirts. He drove them across town and out the other side before pulling into a garage that looked like it had been there since the motor engine had been invented and had not had much done to it since. Rusty signs advertising long forgotten products lined the wall of what looked like a shabby metal shed. But as they grew closer, Rebecca could see it housed the workshop area of the garage. Out front were old-fashioned pumps and a man in a grease stained coverall walked out, wiping his hands on a rag and looked like he was ready to fill the car up. It seemed self service had not reached this far.

Will drove the car past the man standing by the pumps and around to the rear of the shed that served as the car maintenance area.

Here it looked like a graveyard for cars. There were skeletons of cars without wheels, windows and engines, and piles of parts. If there was order to the pile, then Rebecca couldn't work out what it was, but somehow it was what she expected.

Will parked the car at the far end so the vehicle couldn't be seen by anyone but the most curious of visitors. He climbed out, shielding his eyes from the sun, which was now high in the sky.

Rebecca pushed her door open and pulled her feet from the foot well. They seemed to have swollen in the time spent in the car and her legs felt stiff and felt unrelated to her.

Will appeared at her side and held out a hand. She knew she should refuse, but she also doubted she could stand without help. She flashed a quick, grateful smile and took it, allowing Will to steady her as she got to her feet.

Will scanned the yard. Aside from the relics of cars long forgotten, it appeared to be empty.

'This way,' he said, letting go of her hand and walking towards a small back door.

Rebecca's hand seemed to feel the loss of his touch and she wondered if he had picked up on her reluctance. She tried not to think about what conclusions he might have come to. It felt important, but she knew she couldn't let it be, not now, not here.

As quickly as she could she followed Will, suddenly afraid she might lose sight of him. But when he reached the door, he stopped and waited. When Rebecca was by his side he pushed the door open and they stepped into the gloom.

It took Rebecca's eyes a few moments to adjust. It wasn't particularly dark inside but the difference between inside and the bright glare of the sun outside had temporarily blinded her. Will seemed to have no such difficulty as she felt him move away from her. As her eyesight returned she could see that he was crouched down beside a car that had been suspended over a pit.

'Sergeant Anderson. How fares the day?'

It was such an odd thing to say that Rebecca just stared. A deep warm chuckle sounded from the deep pit.

'The day fares well, Lieutenant.'

A figure in a remarkably clean cover-all appeared up the steps from the pit.

Rebecca watched the reunion take place with much back slapping. The sergeant was a tall, black man with a baritone voice.

'It's good to see you, Sir,' Anderson said as he took a step back, looking as if he were standing to attention.

'Enough of that, Pom!' Will said, before he seemed to remember that Rebecca was with him.

'May I introduce Rebecca?'

Rebecca stepped forward, feeling a little shy, and held out her hand. Anderson took it and performed a bow that would not have been out of place in a Jane Austen novel.

'Pleased to meet you,' Rebecca said; following the formal tone of their previous greetings.

Anderson's eyes lit up. 'An English lady! I am honoured,' he beamed.

Rebecca was sure she was missing something.

'Pom is a fan of all things British,' Will explained. 'Not to mention old literature. Would you believe that in his free time he goes to nineteenth-century cotillions?'

Rebecca's eyes widened — while Anderson sounded the part, his profession seemed to be at odds with the idea.

'I know, no one else can believe it either,' he said. 'You could not imagine the ribbing I got for it when the guys found out.'

Anderson gestured to Will who grinned broadly. Anderson sounded so English, if you could ignore the deep south accent.

'I trust this is no social visit?' Anderson said, his face suddenly serious.

'I wish it was, but no. We need a vehicle and I need you to hide the one we came in.'

Rebecca thought he might argue but there was not even a pause.

'Whatever you need, Lieutenant, you know that,' he said.

'I can't really explain . . . ' Will started to say, and Rebecca felt the familiar stab of guilt. He couldn't explain because of her, so he was having to lie by omission to someone who was clearly a trusted friend.

Anderson waved the thought away and walked over to the wall. There was a notice board with nails driven in to it and on it hung a range of car keys. Anderson looked through them and handed a set over to Will.

'Ten-year-old Ford. I take it you want to go unnoticed?' Anderson said.

'Thanks, man,' Will said before stepping in for some more back slapping. Anderson and Will did some complicated handshake fist bump while Rebecca tried not to bounce on the spot with the need to use the facilities.

'The bathroom's through that door over there,' Anderson said pointing to another door. 'Its not posh, but it's clean.' He smiled kindly at her.

Rebecca didn't need to be told twice and she made a dash for the door.

When she returned Will was waiting for her and he had a carrier bag in his hand. He pulled a bottle of water from it and handed it to Rebecca, who took it eagerly.

'Thank you,' she said to Anderson when she had quenched her thirst. 'I know you don't know me but I really appreciate your help.'

'No need. I owe the Lieutenant more than a car and a few supplies.'

The two men locked eyes and something wordless passed between them. Rebecca could only imagine what it was, but whatever it was, it was a bond that ran strong, *as strong as brothers*, she thought.

Anderson led the way out of the shed and round the back. Further on from the car graveyard was a collection of cars that looked as if they might be in working order. Anderson led them to a dark grey Ford that looked as if it would go. It was, as he had said, the kind of car that no one would pay any attention to.

Will climbed in the driver's side and

cranked over the engine. Anderson opened the door for Rebecca so that she could take her seat. When Anderson went to close the door, Rebecca took his hand again.

'Thank you — it's not enough, but thank you,' she told him genuinely, before she climbed into the car and Jack settled in the well at her feet.

'No need, ma'am,' Anderson said, his eyes soft, before he closed the door.

He stood to attention as Will put the car in drive and when Rebecca turned back she could see him standing there until the car turned the corner and he was no longer in sight.

'You could have told him about me,' Rebecca said as the car joined the main road once more. 'You obviously trust him.'

'I trust him with my life,' Will said glancing at her. 'But the less he knows, the better it will be for him if anyone is on our tail.'

The words were so ominous that Rebecca didn't know what to say. How could she respond to that?

Yet again, she had drawn another good person into her drama — and they had helped her, despite the risks. It was too much. She turned her face away from Will and stared out the window as the silent tears fell.

If Will noticed, he said nothing, just let her cry.

They had been on the road for an hour before he spoke again.

'Anderson can look after himself.'

It was a comment that felt as if it had been plucked out of thin air but somehow it managed to answer one of the most pressing questions that was swirling around in Rebecca's head.

'I'm sure he can but that doesn't stop me worrying about it all.'

'Worrying won't change a thing,' Will said. He sounded so much like Peggy that Rebecca had to smile.

'A Peggy-ism,' Will said with a grin.

'I feel like I'm pulling good people into my perfect storm of a life, asking them to take risks when they don't even know me — not to mention the fact that you're pulling in all sorts of favours.'

Will seemed to consider this.

'It's not favours, Rebecca. I would do anything for Anderson, anything he asked of me, whatever the cost. That's not one person owing another until they're even. It's family.'

Rebecca wanted to ask *What about me?*

She had no claim on Will. They had not fought side by side, they did not have the bond of brotherhood, yet she felt a bond all the same. One that she could not describe or explain, even though she had tried to, at least to herself.

Will's dedication to helping her was a mystery, a mystery she was desperate to solve — even if it was not what her heart hoped for. Because at least then she could settle her own feelings and lock them away where they could do no harm to either of them.

11

When they parked up, even knowing that it would make little difference since her understanding of the geography of the US was sketchy at best, nevertheless, Rebecca asked, 'Where are we?'

'Heading to Montana.'

Rebecca had some vague idea that was in the west but that didn't help much either.

'How long till we get there?'

'We're going to have to drive through the night. It's not ideal, I know,' he said, flashing another look at her belly, 'But other than short stops to eat and use facilities, we should keep going.'

'I could drive for a bit. You'll to need to sleep.'

'Not me, used to it from the Army. I'll sleep when we get there.'

They'd pulled into a busy truck stop and eaten some of the food Anderson had sent them off with. It was mainly assorted junk food.

'We'll stop somewhere for hot food later, I promise,' Will said, looking guilty.

'Will, there's no need to apologise. I know you're doing what you think is best and I'm grateful for your help,' Rebecca said, brushing chip crumbs from her front.

She felt a sharp dig in her side and winced, twisting to try and relieve the pain.

Will was at her side in an instant. 'Is it the baby?' he asked, his eyes a little wide with the worry that he didn't seem able to hide.

'It's fine,' Rebecca said, forcing her voice to remain even. 'It's just the baby kicking.' She managed to straighten up and took a deep breath. 'That was a kidney shot,' she said smiling at Will.

He looked at her, his head on one side. She reached out wordlessly for his hand and pulled it towards her belly, placing it over the spot that the last kick had come from. They stood there, suspended in time, and Rebecca wondered if her baby was going to be stubborn, but there was another firm nudge.

Will chuckled. 'Woah, he's a lively one!'

'It might be a girl,' Rebecca said. She wasn't in to any of that nonsense that girls couldn't be as strong as boys.

'I think I would want to know,' Will said thoughtfully. 'I admire your restraint.'

Rebecca didn't know how to explain, knowing that if she tried it would likely shatter the mood and that was the last thing she wanted.

It was not because she was overly traditional, or even that she wanted a surprise. It just hadn't felt right without James — not the man she had come to know he was, but the man she had believed he was. Somehow it hadn't felt right to make that decision without him. Which was strange in itself, since running away to a different country and hiding was probably her most effective step in keeping James's family away from her baby!

Whether she liked it or not the baby

was part of James, and that was something she would always have to live with.

Her mind turned again to how she might explain it to the baby, when he or she was old enough. Rebecca could only hope she could make them understand, that she had done everything to protect them from a life that she couldn't bear them to be exposed to.

Rebecca's mind was brought back to the present by a car drawing up and parking next to them. A family climbed out and walked over to the toilets, and Rebecca remembered where she was and what they needed to do.

'We should go,' she said, and her focus returned to Will who was looking at her thoughtfully.

He couldn't read her mind — she knew that, of course — but somehow he gave the impression that he knew what she was thinking.

He nodded wordlessly and whistled for Jack, who had been off relieving himself in the scrubland beside the road.

Will climbed back into the car. Rebecca took one last look at the family walking away from her and once more silently apologised to her baby. She knew it was the right choice, that it had been the only choice, but still, she was keeping the baby from any family — her own, not to mention the Barters. *Some day, we'll see my side of the family. Some day when it's safe.*

Rebecca swallowed the lump that had appeared in her throat. Would it ever be safe? She had no idea. That thought wrapped her in a cloak of loneliness that made her want to just curl up in a ball and cry.

★   ★   ★

Rebecca had closed her eyes and slept. Jack had rested his head on her lap and it was strangely comforting. It seemed the only thing she could do to escape her thoughts and fears.

Will had woken her after a while so that they could eat. He had bought takeaway food from a diner and they had eaten it in silence, leaning against the car.

As soon as they were finished, they hit the road again.

Rebecca felt as if she was trapped in the car, as if the four sides were pressing in on her and she would suffocate, but the car moved on and the distance between them and Blowing Rock grew ever greater.

The sun rose early over the flat landscape and they continued on.

By late afternoon, Rebecca was starting to feel like they were as far away from civilisation as it was possible to be. She could not remember the last time she had seen a building, let alone other people. The road itself was deserted and started to take on an almost post-apocalyptic feel.

She moved in her seat, trying to stretch out the stiffness in her back and regain some feeling in her legs.

Will seemed focused and yet relaxed, as if he were in some kind of zone.

Rebecca felt more than a little jealous that he was dealing with everything so well, but then it sounded as if he had plenty of experience — not to mention the fact that he wasn't pregnant or on the run from a family involved heavily in organised crime.

Rebecca looked across at him. Technically he was on the run too. She still hadn't figured out how that had happened. She wondered how he'd managed to arrange the time off of work.

Will took a turn to the left and they were heading through wide open plains. The more miles they moved, the more desolate it seemed to get.

'We should be there in another thirty,' Will said suddenly, breaking the silence.

'Does your friend know we're coming?' Rebecca asked.

Will chuckled. 'No way to tell 'em. They don't have a phone or internet and they collect their post once a month from a post office box.'

Rebecca raised an eyebrow. That

seemed unusual, if not downright paranoid.

'That's off-grid,' Will said, seeing her expression. 'They wouldn't even do that if they could get away from the tax man,' he added, grinning.

'Sounds like a good place to hide out.'

'I wouldn't be taking you there if it wasn't.'

'If they live off-grid like this, how will they feel about unexpected visitors?'

'Oh, they won't much like it at first, but they'll soon get over it.'

That, Rebecca thought, was not comforting. It was bad enough asking for help from people who were willing to give it, but she couldn't imagine how uncomfortable it would be to be thrust upon people who had made life choices to live apart from the rest of the world.

'Don't look so worried. They're good people.'

Rebecca didn't like to point out that these words didn't exactly match with the large sign they had just passed

— signs that, in no uncertain words, made it horribly clear what would happened to trespassers and other uninvited guests. They were set with such regularity along the dusty road that Rebecca was sure that visitors might have once ignored the first few and so the owners of the land had felt the need to remind people every hundred metres or so!

Will pulled up at a gate. It was heavy metal and at least six feet tall, the top covered with angry-looking barbed wire. The gate linked into a steel fence of the same height that ran off in both directions as far as Rebecca could see.

He climbed out of the car and Rebecca joined him. It was an excuse to stretch her legs but also to ask what they were going to do now.

When she reached Will's side she saw that he was waving at the sky with a funny looking grin on his face. Rebecca wondered briefly if he had finally lost the plot, maybe due to sleep deprivation, but then she heard a metal whir and saw that a security camera set on top of the gate was now moving in their direction.

Rebecca had no idea what the protocol was when you are being checked out a security camera. She looked up and tried out a smile but that felt both silly and ridiculous considering the circumstances, not to mention the fact that she didn't really feel she had much to smile about.

Every time she thought about what her life had become she couldn't quite believe it. It seemed wild, like a nightmare where your mind pulls in all sorts of different elements to make a dream that barely makes any sense. Yet here she was, hoping to find shelter with people who had chosen to cut themselves off from the world.

Rebecca had once watched a programme about so called 'doomsday preppers' and they had all seemed a little strange, and that was putting it politely. Still, a small part of her had always wondered if they knew something she didn't.

The metal gate started to open and that brought Rebecca back to the here and now. It didn't swing open but instead slid back along the fence, reminding Rebecca of a prison gate.

Will was already in the car when she climbed back in. 'Well, they're letting us in, which is a good sign.'

Rebecca turned to stare at him. He said nothing when he took in her expression as if he believed what he had just said was entirely reasonable.

'Was there ever a doubt?' Rebecca couldn't believe they had driven non-stop for several days on the offchance that an old friend might let them onto his property.

Will just shrugged. 'They're great people, but they aren't that keen on strangers.'

Rebecca stared blankly out of the side window. Who knew what they were going to make of a pregnant woman who was going to bring trouble to their home?

'What makes you think they'll let us

stay once you tell them why we're here?' She didn't add that your average person might baulk at the idea of bringing that kind of trouble to the place where they lived — let alone people who seemed to have turned paranoia into a work of art.

'Relax. Like I said, they're good people.'

Rebecca was not reassured by this, not one bit. She didn't think she could face being turned away and rejected. Where would they go then?

She was desperate to feel safe, to find somewhere she could sleep and recover a little from the events of the last few days. Her emotions felt ragged and she didn't think any of this would be good for her blood pressure or the health of her baby.

The dusty road ran through what looked like meadow and pasture. In the distance Rebecca could make out a herd of animals — cattle, she thought — but they were far enough away to make it difficult to tell.

Will brought the car to a stop in front of another set of gates. This time the fence was wooden, but again it was topped with angry-looking barbed wire and Rebecca could see cameras again. This time Will didn't get out of the car and the gate opened to let them through.

He drove the car up through some outbuildings, past a large barn, and up to a house that looked exactly as Rebecca had imagined a farmhouse in the midwest to look. It was made entirely of wood, which had weathered to a beautiful pinky grey. The sloping roof had a chimney and smoke filtered gently into the air. On the front door was a wreath made of autumn leaves and the whole image was one of frontier living from a time long forgotten. There was a porch that ran the full length of the front of the house and there were chairs and a rocker placed at intervals, with piles of home-made blankets, ready for people to enjoy the view. A tall flag pole stood proudly beside the house with an American flag flapping in the wind.

Will climbed out of the car and walked round to Rebecca's side, opening her door. Jack jumped out and sat waiting. Will helped her to lever herself out. She wasn't sure if it was the long drive or the fact that with each day her baby was growing bigger, but it was definitely getting harder to manoeuvre herself.

She had barely got both feet on the ground when the front door opened. A man walked down the front steps and his appearance was so startling that for a moment Rebecca forgot herself and stared.

The man didn't seem to notice — or if he did, he gave the impression he was used to it and it didn't really matter to him.

Instead he strode towards Will and pulled him into a back-slapping hug. 'Lieutenant.'

'How many times have I told you to call me Will?' His voice was light with amusement.

'And you can keep on telling me, that's a habit I'm not willing to break.'

The two men locked arms and looked at each other. Will seem totally unfazed by his friend's appearance and Rebecca suspected that had been a hard-won event. The man's face looked as if it had been worked over with sand paper. There was no smoothness, only scars and wrinkled skin, like a patchwork of fields seen from above.

'Rebecca, allow me to introduce Marshall King. We all call him HRH.'

Rebecca smiled and stepped forward offering out a hand to shake.

Marshall took it and shook it gently, ducking his head. 'A real pleasure to meet you, Rebecca.'

'Sorry for turning up unexpectedly,' Will said and was rewarded by a booming laugh.

'Unexpected is about the only way, unless you plan months in advance. Now come with me, you both look like you could do with a drink and something to eat. Martha will have my hide if I leave you out here any longer.'

Marshall held out his hand and directed them to the front door.

The kitchen ran the whole length of the back of the house. It contained two wood-burning stoves and a rustic-looking wooden trestle table that looked large enough to seat at least twenty.

A black and white cat was curled up on top of one of the stoves, and the dog beds arranged around the open fire suggested that the feline was not the only pet.

Jack trotted over to a water bowl and had a long, noisy drink before settling himself into one of the dog baskets.

An older woman in jeans and a check shirt was pouring an old-fashioned black kettle.

'Now, Marshall. I told you not to leave our guests standing around out-side, especially when not when one looks ready to fall down.'

'Sorry, ma'am,' Marshall said. 'Will, you remember Martha, my mother-in-law?'

Will grinned as he enveloped Martha in a hug.

'You promised you were going to visit with us,' Martha said, trying to sound mighty put out.

'Well, here I am,' Will said, releasing Martha from the hug and holding his arms wide.

Martha looked other than impressed. 'You made that promise nigh on two years ago, boy.'

'Yes, ma'am, but work . . . '

Martha cut him off with a wave of his hand and turned her attention to Rebecca.

'Now, my dear, come and sit down. I imagine you could do with taking the weight off.'

Rebecca found herself led by the hand to a rocking chair and before she could protest she had a blanket over her knees and a mug of something hot in her hand.

'No caffeine for you. That's herbal tea. I grow the herbs and dry them myself. A recipe from my grandmother

— will do you the world of good after your long trip.'

Rebecca wasn't keen on herbal tea but since she had found out she was pregnant that seemed to be the only thing she was ever offered. Martha was a fierce but kind woman and was clearly used to everyone — including her burly son-in-law — doing as she told them to. So Rebecca took a sip meekly and was pleasantly surprised — it had a fruity taste and was actually not bad at all.

Martha raised an eyebrow and gave her a knowing smile, as if she knew exactly what Rebecca had been thinking.

Will and Marshall had taken a seat at the table and Martha poured them coffee from a pot, then one for herself, taking a seat opposite them.

Rebecca sipped her tea and watched as they caught up on all the latest family news.

For the first time since leaving town, she was starting to feel relaxed. She found herself thinking that perhaps they would be safe here — at least for a while, anyway.

Her mind wandered as she allowed herself to imagine setting up a life here, even raising her baby here, safely away from the rest of the world.

The only problem with the daydream was that Will's face appeared in every picture. The truth was, she couldn't imagine taking that step — assuming she would even be welcome to stay that long — without him.

And that was something she could never ask of him. Having established that his top motivations in life were duty and honour, he might agree based solely on that. So she knew she could never ask him.

She shook her head, trying to rid her mind of the ideas and the images that came with them. She didn't have time for fairytales. She needed to focus on today, and maybe tomorrow. There was too much at stake and too much danger all around her to do anything but that.

The conversation at the table had

turned to the matter at hand, and Rebecca listened as Will succinctly told her tale. It seemed strange to hear someone else talk through all that had happened to her, but somehow it was a comfort too.

'So you'll be needing somewhere to stay,' Marshall said, and Rebecca watched as he exchanged glances with Martha. Rebecca couldn't read the meaning of the look and her stomach dropped at the thought of having to head back out into the world out there.

'Just for a little while,' Will said. Rebecca couldn't tell if he was concerned or not.

Just then, the back door opened and a woman walked in. She was maybe ten years older than Rebecca and had the look of someone who worked the land and didn't care much for her appearance. Despite that, she was breathtakingly beautiful. Marshall stood up and leaned in to kiss her. The contrast in their faces was distinct.

'No guests but family, and certainly

no strangers,' the woman said, fixing Marshall with a hard stare. 'Those are the rules we all agreed.'

Rebecca felt as if the world had tilted on its axis. All thoughts of a break from the stress of her life were gone. The image of her and the baby being safe had shattered like a pane of glass that had been dropped.

She was going to have to head out again — and to where, she had no idea.

12

Martha started to speak, holding out a placating hand. 'Now, honey . . . '

'No, Ma, you know the rules.'

'But these are extenuating circumstances,' Martha said.

'I'm mighty sorry to hear of your troubles,' the woman said, looking to Will and then Rebecca. 'But this is our safe haven and we've given enough.' The woman's eyes traced the pattern of burned skin on her husband's face. 'We've no more to give. You're welcome to stay for supper, but then I must ask you to be on your way.'

The woman looked at her feet and then with some effort she said, 'I'm going to wash up and round up the kids, and then I'll come give you a hand to prepare supper.'

Everyone watched her go and then it was as if they had all been holding their breath. There was silence and it seemed like no one knew what to say to break it.

'Gaby seems well,' Will said finally, which seemed like a strange statement to Rebecca.

'She has good days and bad days,' Marshall said, and the pain of whatever it was seemed to cross his face.

'That kind of loss is not easily borne by any of us,' Martha said, topping up the coffee before getting to her feet and starting to load logs into one of the wood burning stoves.

'We lost our daughter, Chelsea,' Marshall said, the words catching in his throat. 'Terrorism. She was only nine.'

Rebecca felt as if she had been punched. The idea of losing her baby was unbearable to her, and the thought of having to live with that loss every day was too much. Her ragged emotions betrayed her and tears started to flow.

'That's how I got my scars. I was there with her, at the race. I survived and Chelsea didn't.' He shook his head at the memory and Will placed a hand on his shoulder.

'I should have thought, man. I'm so sorry.'

'Gaby is a wonderful woman,' Marshall said as if he needed to explain. 'She would do anything for anyone, but right now she can't see beyond her own family. Everything outside this place is a terrible risk to her.'

'I understand,' Rebecca said and then silently cursing herself added, 'I don't mean to presume . . . ' feeling if it were at all possible, that she was making the situation worse.

'Mothers understand, even those who've yet to meet their babes,' Martha said with a sad smile.

'We should be going,' Rebecca said trying to stand up quickly and failing.

'You sit yourself back down,' Martha said sternly. 'We'll have food first and then we'll be thinking about how we can help you.'

'But . . . ' Rebecca started to protest until she saw the look on Martha's face.

Rebecca stayed where she was but all she wanted to do was run. Everywhere she went she brought pain and upset, not to mention danger, and now she was doing it here.

Once more she thought about whether she should go it alone, although how she would convince Will, she had no idea. One thing she was sure of, they couldn't stay here. She couldn't — no, wouldn't — be responsible for bringing more pain to this family than they had already suffered.

A church-style bell was rung outside, and Rebecca began to understand the need for such a large table as people seemed to simply pour into the kitchen.

Rebecca was introduced to each one but she wasn't sure she would be able to remember everyone's name. There were four children, all of primary school age, among them. Two were Gaby and Marshall's, the other two belonged to Gaby's brother, who also lived on the homestead. The adults were relatives or family friends of many years. It seemed it was very much a family business and a tight community here.

Rebecca had been dreading meeting the others, worried that her and Will's presence would cause more upset and even some suspicion, but her concerns were unfounded as everyone seemed pleased to have them there and they were both greeted warmly as if they were old friends.

The conversation at supper seemed to revolve around the tasks that needed to be completed the following day and a report on how well the children had done at school. Although it was a much smaller gathering, it reminded Rebecca painfully of Blowing Rock. It was the kind of environment she wanted to raise her child in, especially considering there could be no family involved, but again, it seemed beyond her grasp.

*   *   *

Supper broke up early but then Rebecca suspected the days here started around dawn so early nights were essential. In the end only Marshall, Gaby, Martha, Will and Rebecca were left at the long table.

'I've been thinking,' Martha said, and all eyes turned to look at her. Gaby looked reproachful, as if she was worried Martha was about to try and convince her to change her mind. 'About the old Jones homestead,' Martha said. Rebecca saw some of the tension in Gaby's shoulders lessen. 'No one would think to look for you there. Only the folks here would even know you were there. It's basic but we could make it homely enough.'

'It's on the edge of the property, about ten miles out,' Marshall said. 'We would be the nearest neighbours, so Martha's right — no one would ever think to look for you there. We don't own it but no one really does since old Jonesy passed. We use it if we're running cattle out on the western edge. Its boundaries rest up against the national park.'

Marshall looked to his wife and took her hand in his. It was clear he was only going to move forward with this new plan if Gaby could cope with the idea. Gaby looked to her husband and then her mother, before turning her gaze on Rebecca.

If you had told Rebecca a month ago that she would be hoping against hope that she could stay in a run-down cabin in the middle of the wilderness, she would have laughed, but right now it seemed the best option.

Will looked to Rebecca, who nodded wordlessly.

'Are you sure? I would understand if you want us both gone.'

There was silence as Marshall and Gaby had a conversation without words. Rebecca closed her eyes. She couldn't imagine where they would go if they had to leave. Perhaps Will had some other plan up his sleeve but he seemed as keen to stay as she did.

'You can stay at the old cabin,' Gaby said slowly. 'But make your way there tonight.'

Rebecca looked out of the windows. The sun was already on its way to setting and in this part of the world, when it disappeared, total darkness fell immediately. But she knew they were lucky that Gaby had agreed to the plan and under the circumstances Rebecca couldn't blame her. After all, she was running from something similar.

Rebecca had known that if she had stayed in England she would eventually lose her child — not in the same way as Gaby and Marshall had, but lost all the same. There was no way she could be sure that her child would be kept safe from the life that had consumed its father.

Rebecca looked up and realised that Will, Marshall and Martha were already galvanised into action, bustling around the kitchen loading up supplies from the ample pantry.

Rebecca made to stand up but a look from Gaby told her to stay where she was.

'We'll get everything you need,' Gaby said before turning away. 'It's the least we can do.'

Rebecca watched Gaby's retreating back, knowing that the woman was battling with conflicting emotions. She sighed. She was causing yet more pain and no doubt the associated guilt when Gaby had nothing to feel that way for, and it was all Rebecca's fault. The only thing she could do was leave and never come back, to leave the family in peace as they tried to continue their healing. Rebecca had been so relieved to arrive but now all she wanted to do was leave.

She heard the front door open and the sound of voices talking softly as the car was loaded with supplies and she felt useless, not even allowed to help out in a small way. It was not a feeling she was used to. She was normally fiercely independent but it seemed like the Barter family had somehow stolen that from her, too.

Just the thought of them fuelled her simmering anger and she stood up. Everyone was being very kind but she was pregnant, not sick, and she was still capable of making a contribution.

Martha glanced at her but seemed able to read her expression and handed her a pile of blankets to carry out to the car. The back seat was stuffed full of boxes up to the ceiling and Will and Marshall were standing by the car, talking. They stopped as Rebecca approached and she felt another flash of annoyance. Anything they had to say, they could say in front of her, since all this was about her and her baby.

'Martha says this is the last of it,' Rebecca said, looking from Marshall to Will.

'We should head off then,' Will said taking the blankets from her and managing to shove them into the last remaining space in the back. 'I can't thank you enough, man — and I'm sorry if we've brought upset.'

Marshall took Will's hand and they shook before doing a man hug with back slapping.

'I'm sorry we can't do more.' He looked as if he were about to try and explain again but Will waved it away.

'I should have thought. And we're grateful for all you've done. Hopefully we won't need the cabin for more than a couple of weeks.'

'You take care,' Marshall said, turning to Rebecca with an apologetic smile.

Rebecca threw her arms around his neck — so unlike her but she couldn't think of any other way to tell him she understood and he had nothing to feel bad about. Considering the circumstances, the fact that they had been able to help as much as they had was more than she could expect.

'Thank you for everything, and you take care of your family,' she said softly before breaking away from him.

She was rewarded with a less apologetic smile and couldn't shake the thought that both Marshall and Gaby would no doubt reproach themselves for sending Rebecca away, but she didn't know how to explain to them that she understood more than they knew.

Will had opened the car door for her to climb in and so she did. There was nothing more to be said and their continued presence meant an increased likelihood that they would bring danger to this safe haven.

Marshall and Will exchanged a few words and again Rebecca couldn't hear what was being said but as Will climbed in the car, Jack jumped into Will's lap and then settled himself in the footwell at Rebecca's feet. She decided she would ask Will what they were discussing later. Will's face was solemn and she knew he was feeling guilty for bringing her here.

Rebecca's life felt like a set of dominoes. The first one had been knocked down by the revelation that the man she loved was not who she thought he was and the impact of that was now spreading, knocking over dominoes even on the other side of the world, affecting people who had experienced tragedy beyond her worst nightmares.

The dilemma remained, though. How could she keep her baby safe without help, without dragging innocent people into her fight?

'The road will take us so far and then we'll have to go over some pretty rough ground. The car's not designed for it, so it's not going to be a smooth ride,' Will spoke into the darkness, but his eyes were fixed on the dusty track ahead — Rebecca didn't think it qualified as a road.

'I'm just grateful we have somewhere to stay.' She wanted to add 'that will be safe' but if she was honest, she wasn't sure that was true. Was anywhere safe from the reach of the Barter family? She'd thought leaving the country would have been enough, but they had tracked her down easily and their reach seemed to take in the American authorities.

She shuddered at the thought.

'Are you cold?' Will asked. 'I can stop and get a blanket out?'

'I'm fine, just thinking.'

'Care to share?'

Rebecca thought about this for a moment.

'You first.'

It came out more petulantly than she

had planned. She was tired — no, exhausted — and worn out by the fear and uncertainty, but she knew she had no right to take it out on Will, who had put everything on the line for her when he barely knew her.

'Sorry,' she added quickly.

'No need. I understand you're frustrated but right now I'll like to concentrate on getting safely to the cabin. Once we're set up, we can get some sleep and talk about everything in the morning.'

Rebecca wanted to demand that he tell her right now, but she knew he was making a sensible suggestion. She was exhausted but she couldn't work out when Will had last been able to get some sleep, and so it would be beyond unfair for her to suggest an alternative plan.

'That sounds good,' she said, wondering whether she would be able to sleep. Every bone in her body was begging for rest but she suspected her mind would have other ideas.

Will hadn't been exaggerating; the

journey was rough. At times Rebecca thought the car wouldn't make it and they would be stuck out in the wilderness, but Will skilfully navigated every dip, slope and hole and somehow managed to keep them moving forward.

When the car's headlights lit up the cabin, Rebecca had to fight not to cry, she was so relieved. It was really little more than a wooden shack but right now it looked like the Hilton.

Will pushed open the door — it seemed that there were no locks — and shone a torch around the inside. His torch settled on an oil lamp and he pulled a box of matches from his pocket and lit it. The light was dim but the room was small, so light spilled into all but the darkest corners.

It was one single room, with a wood burning stove that doubled as a cooker and the only heat source. There was a rickety double bed that looked old enough to be an antique, and a handmade table and chairs, and that was it.

Rebecca could see no other doors

that might lead to other important rooms, like a bathroom.

'It's an outhouse, I'm afraid,' Will said.

Rebecca shouldn't have been surprised. It wasn't as if people who lived this far out were connected to mains electricity and had indoor plumbing. Still, being pregnant and having to find her way outside in the dark to use the facilities did not fill her with anything other than dread.

Will returned from the car with the first box of supplies. 'Martha included a Thermos of hot water, so we can make a hot drink for now. It's going to take a while to get the fire going. Do you mind doing the honours?'

Jack trotted round the cabin giving everything a good sniff and Rebecca was once more grateful that she had been able to bring the dog with her.

By the time Will unloaded the car, Rebecca was standing ready with a tin mug of coffee for him and a mug of Martha's herbal tea for her. They sat down at the table and Rebecca wondered when the issue of the bed was going to be discussed.

'Marshall loaned me a sleeping bag so I can sleep on the floor,' Will said, once again showing an uncanny ability to read her mind.

'You don't need to do that. We're both grown-ups. I'm sure we can cope with sharing a bed.' Despite her best efforts, Rebecca could feel some colour rise in her cheeks and could only hope that the dim light would hide her embarrassment. 'I mean, the floor doesn't look comfortable or particularly clean.' Rebecca knew she was rambling but couldn't help herself.

'I've slept on a lot worse,' Will said with a grin that suggested he had seen her blush.

Rebecca would never say it, not out loud at least, but she almost wished he would agree to share the bed. She wasn't expecting anything to happen, of course not, but the idea of having a person close enough for her to reach out and touch was a comforting thought. She tried to shake the image from her mind but it seemed determined to cling on.

'I'm happy to do whatever you want,' Will said in a casual tone.

Rebecca felt heat pass up through her and so she stood up abruptly and turned away. 'I just don't want you to be uncomfortable.'

She winced as she realised that could be taken either way. What was she doing? Will had no doubt slept in worse places than the floor of a rundown cabin, so why was she making such a fuss? She couldn't bear to turn and see his face.

'How do I find the outhouse?' she said. She would need to go before bed but she wasn't desperate, yet it seemed the only way to shift the conversation.

'I'll come with you.'

Now Rebecca did turn round, eyebrows raised.

'Snakes,' Will said. 'And coyotes.'

Rebecca had no idea if what he had

said was true but he sounded like the serious Will she had come to know. Most importantly the embarrassing topic of the bed seemed to have been dropped.

'Thanks,' Rebecca said, not knowing what else you were supposed to say to someone who was escorting you to the toilet to protect you from local wildlife.

Will picked up the lantern, reached into one of the boxes and pulled out a shotgun. Rebecca took a step back. The only people she ever saw carrying any kind of gun were armed police — and they weren't that common, even in London.

'Marshall gave it to me, to keep the vermin away,' Will said.

It was only when Rebecca followed him out of the door that she had time to consider what sort of vermin he was referring to. Rebecca had known that Will carried a gun — his Sheriff uniform came with a handgun — but to see him with a shotgun made her feel like he was preparing for some sort of battle. It sent a shiver down her spine that the danger so great that they might need weapons to protect themselves!

She stood on the doorstep unable to make her feet move. Will's hand appeared in the gloom and she looked into his face. His expression was solemn but somehow his presence gave her the courage and she took his hand and allowed herself to be led out into the night.

13

When Rebecca woke, she felt bathed in sunlight, as if she had chosen to sleep outdoors in the wilderness. She pulled the blankets up to her chin and forced her eyes to open.

There was a lump under the covers next to her, which snuffled in sleep. Apparently Jack had not been content with sleeping on top of the blankets. She reached a hand under the layers and stroked his ears. She probably should have been cross but since he was functioning as a very efficient hot water bottle she couldn't really complain. Besides, his nearness was a comfort.

Will was in the area that could be classed as a kitchen and was pushing logs into the wood burning stove.

'Morning. It should warm up in an hour or so. I'll bring you hot tea once I've got this going.'

Rebecca didn't think she had the energy to argue and so instead she shuffled upright in the bed, pulling the blankets with her and had a proper look at her new home.

It was sparse. The people who had previously owned the place had not shown any flair for decoration or even personalisation — there were no pictures or photographs on the rough wooden walls. Aside from the boxes they'd brought, the place looked as if it had been abandoned — which Rebecca guessed it had, except for occasional use by Marshall and his family.

Will walked over with two mugs of steaming liquid and Rebecca shifted so he could sit on the edge of the bed. They hadn't discussed the bed issue any further the night before. Will had simply unrolled his sleeping bag and settled down for the night. Rebecca eyed the floor and wondered if she should suggest that he took the bed that night, but she knew he would say no. She couldn't imagine him sleeping in a bed and letting the pregnant woman sleep on the floor.

'How are you feeling?' Will asked and his eyes strayed to her belly which was almost hidden under the pile of blankets.

Right at that moment, Jack wriggled up the bed so his head appeared. Rebecca and Will laughed as Jack let his tongue loll out.

'I'm fine . . . we're fine,' she said with a small smile. The baby had been moving around all night. It was like that sometimes, and she felt sure that he or she only slept when she was awake. 'Can you tell me what the plan is?'

Will took a sip of coffee and Rebecca got the distinct impression she wasn't going to like whatever he was about to say.

'Once I've got everything set up for you, I'm going to have to head off.'

Rebecca stared. He couldn't honestly think that he was going to abandon her to fend for herself, here in the middle of nowhere? She was a city girl, born and bred, and had no idea about things like keeping fires going. And that was before she even let herself think about finding her way to the outhouse by herself. She could take Jack with her of course, but she didn't want him trying to fight off any wildlife that might approach and end up getting hurt. She didn't think she could bear that.

'I wouldn't unless it was absolutely necessary. I had hoped you could stay with Marshall but I didn't really think that through.'

He looked like he was beating himself up about that. Rebecca knew he was right — she didn't like it, but unless they planned on living out here for the rest of their lives, then she needed to at least listen to his plan.

'It's OK, I'll be fine. I've got Jack for company.' Rebecca tried to force some cheerfulness into her voice but to her own ears she sounded slightly hysterical. Jack didn't help the impression by wriggling up next to her and starting to whimper.

'I'll just be a day and a night, no

longer,' Will said and as he looked at her it was clear that he too was doubting the sense in leaving her alone.

'I can manage,' Rebecca said, already wondering whether she should ask for a quick lesson in firing a shotgun and whether she would ever feel like she could use it. She was not a fan of guns. Although she understood that people on farms might need them, she couldn't ever see herself firing a gun — not at an animal and definitely not at a person. However, perhaps knowing how to use one would make her feel less frightened of being alone.

'Where are you going?' Rebecca didn't want to dwell on what she would do when he left; instead she wanted to focus on the plan that Will seemed to think might give her and the baby a chance to be free of the Barter family forever.

'I put some feelers out to people I can trust. I haven't mentioned your identity or anything to do with you, but I wanted to gauge what kind of interest there might be in information against the Barter family.'

Rebecca swallowed. 'I don't have any.' She could hear the despair in her own voice. 'I was kept out of things, and as soon as I discovered who James was, I left. I haven't even met his family. He told me they lived abroad. Of course that's not true, nothing about him was true.'

'My plan wasn't to involve you, Rebecca. My suggestion is that we set a trap for the people who have been employed to find you. They're bound to be well known to the authorities here in the US, which is the carrot my contact may need, and if we play our cards right they might lead us to back to the Barter family themselves.'

Rebecca couldn't see how any of that would help in the long term. It might get the current people off her trail but surely the Barters would send more?

'Sometimes when you pull on a thread it all starts to unravel. If we can put pressure on the right people, they might be prepared to rat out on the Barters.'

Rebecca couldn't imagine anyone the Barter family employed would be so quick to give up information, but then she didn't know much about how these things worked. Unless you counted movies and TV shows as accurate portrayals of crime families.

She wasn't sure it was sensible to hope that Will might be right, to hope he might be able to pull off this plan. Most of all to hope that one day she might be free to live her life not in hiding.

She watched Will as he set about unpacking the rest of the supplies.

Was it right to hope that she might even find love again? Was it selfish to put her own needs and wants anywhere on her list of priorities? Surely right now, it should be all about the baby?

But children need a father figure, and Will would be perfect. The thought slipped into her mind before she could censor it and it was difficult, painful even, to push it away. He was helping her, but that was about duty, not affection — and it wouldn't be fair to

Will to project her own feelings onto him. No, he had given enough, and to ask more of him was not fair. Besides, she wouldn't want him to stay because he felt duty bound.

No — if she was to find love again, then it would be love on both sides, not duty.

'Sorry?' she said when she realised Will was talking to her.

'I asked if you wanted breakfast in bed,' Will said, not looking at her but focusing on the eggs he was scrambling in a heavy pan on the stove.

'No thanks, I need to go and use the facilities.'

'Just give me a minute and I'll come with you.'

'No need,' Rebecca said swinging her legs out of bed. 'I'll need to go on my own while you're away. I'll yell if anything happens.'

'At least take Jack with you.'

'I don't want him getting bitten by a snake.'

'He's sensible enough to smell them

coming, he's a mountain dog,' Will said.

Rebecca looked as Jack trotted over to the door and sat patiently waiting. His expression suggested that he thought she was the one who needed to be kept safe, so Rebecca opened the door and Jack led the way.

★   ★   ★

When they returned, Will had breakfast laid out on the table. She took her seat with Jack by her side. Will pushed a tin bowl in Jack's direction and he fell on it as if he'd not been fed for days.

'He needs to work on his table manners,' Will said with a grin.

Rebecca laughed. 'I don't think you can change him now,' she said.

Jack had wolfed down his food and was now eyeing the bacon and egg on their plates with a greedy stare. Rebecca tore off a piece of bacon and tossed it into his bowl.

'We have food and staples for a week at least. I'll show you the water pump out back. Marshall says the water tastes of minerals but it's safe to drink. All the same, I'll make sure I bring back some bottled water.'

Rebecca nodded. 'Can I ask where you're going?' she said.

'Heading back the way we came. As soon as I'm back in cell phone reception I can check my emails. I've told my contact it's urgent, so I should be able to meet up quickly and then get back to you.'

It all seemed tenuous to Rebecca. What if Will's contact was out of the country? What if they weren't interested? Then what would they do? She couldn't expect Will to hide out in this cabin for the rest of his life — any more than she thought she could survive and bring up a baby out here all by herself.

'It's just the first step, Rebecca. If this doesn't work we'll come up with another plan.'

'If this doesn't work, I don't think I can ask you to do any more,' Rebecca said. She knew she needed to say it. She needed to give him an out, even though she couldn't imagine what she would do or where she would go without him.

'You didn't ask,' Will said as if it was nothing. 'I told you I would help you and your baby and that's what I'm doing. Once this is over and we know you and the little one will be safe, well then, you can decide what you want to do next.'

Will stood up abruptly and collected their plates before moving to the small sink. It had no taps, but it did have a drain. Will poured water from the kettle and started to wash up.

Rebecca knew that she couldn't trust her internal emotion detector right now so she tried to ignore her mind's interpretation of Will's words and actions. Was he trying to subtly tell her that he would like to be a part of her future? Her mind replayed his words and she shook her head. She was imagining it; she was reading too much into words which could be taken a number of ways.

Maybe he was saying he would gladly

let her go off to some other part of the world and let her start her life anew?

None of this was helping and so she got to her feet and pulled a tea towel from a nearby box and started to dry up. She expected Will to protest and tell her to sit down but maybe he realised that she needed to do something.

★   ★   ★

An hour later, Will was packed up and ready to leave. He seemed as reluctant to leave her as she was to see him go, but they both knew he needed to, unless they planned to hide out in the cabin for the rest of their lives. While there were aspects of that which could be considered appealing, overall Rebecca knew it was not a practical option.

Will had checked and triple-checked everything in the small cabin. He had shown her how to keep the fire going, how to relight it should it go out, and given her a brief tutorial on how to fire the shotgun, which Rebecca still wasn't sure she would ever be able to bring herself to use.

There was nothing else to be done, except to say goodbye.

When Will had checked the cabin's supply of firewood for what must be the tenth time, Rebecca knew she needed to do something.

'My grandad use to say the sooner you leave, the sooner you'll be back.'

Will stopped counting the log pile and turned to face her.

'He was a wise man,' Will said. 'Just now I'm faced with it, I can see all the flaws in my plan to leave a pregnant lady alone in the wilderness.'

'You don't think I can look after myself?' Rebecca said crossing her arms and raising an eyebrow. It was all bravado, of course. Normally she would say she was perfectly capable of looking after herself, but to say she was out of her element in the cabin was an understatement.

'I wouldn't dream of making such a suggestion,' Will said, holding his hands out in front of him, as if he was trying to calm down a hostage taker.

Rebecca wasn't sure if he bought her bravado or if he was just going along with it to make them both feel better.

'I suspect that's my cue to take my leave.'

He walked over to the door and opened it. Jack jumped off the bed and came to lean against Rebecca's leg.

'I'll be as quick as I can,' he said, some of the concern back in his voice.

'I know you will,' Rebecca said walking towards the door.

Will was now on the steps but didn't look as if he could move any further away.

'It's OK,' she said stepping close to him and putting her arms around him.

She was trying to comfort him, she told herself. Will's arms encircled her and she could feel his heart beating in his chest.

It took all her reserves of strength not to beg him to stay, despite all the reasons she knew he had to go. Will didn't seem to want to let go of her either.

Finally it was the baby that made them step back from each other.

'Woah! That's quite a kick,' Will said, staring at Rebecca's belly with a look of wonder in his eyes. 'It seems I've been given my marching orders,' he said, locking his eyes on Rebecca in such a way that she didn't think she would ever be able to look away.

'Stay in the cabin and keep warm,' he said.

'You be careful too,' Rebecca said, her mind turning to thoughts of what could happen to Will out there. What if the people hired by the Barter family knew who he was — and knew he was helping her?

'I think I can manage a meeting with an old contact.'

'That's not the bit I'm worried about.'

'I was an Army Ranger. I can handle myself.' Will said it in such a way that it wasn't a boast but more of a statement of fact.

'On a battlefield, yes, but these people don't play by the rules.' Rebecca didn't really know that but she knew enough to suspect it was true.

'I'll be back before you know it,' Will said.

This time he pulled the car door open and climbed in. He wound down the window and held up his hand.

Rebecca watched him drive away, trying to ignore the overwhelming fear that she was never going to see him again.

* * *

It had been a long day by the time Rebecca got into bed. The sun had only just set but despite the fire the temperature had dropped and it seemed the warmest, not to mention safest, place to be.

She had found a book in one of the boxes. It was a historical romance, not the sort of thing that she normally would chose to read, but at least it was something to pass the hours.

Jack was curled up beside her and she

was dreading the need to go out and use the outhouse in the dark, all the while knowing there was no way she could put it off until it was light again in the morning — maybe she could have before the baby, but certainly not while she was pregnant.

'We'll give it another hour and then I'll make a dash for it,' she told Jack, who just looked at her and yawned. Then he tilted his head to one side. Rebecca smiled and reached out a hand to stroke his ears but Jack flew off the bed.

For a second Rebecca thought she had hurt him — but then she realised that he had heard something!

As she moved to lever herself out of bed, she realised that she had heard something, too . . .

14

Jack was scrabbling at the door but there was no way that Rebecca was going to let him out. She leaned against the wall and peered through one of the small windows. She could make out little in the darkness, and the moon seemed to be hidden behind thick clouds.

Suddenly two points of lights appeared, swerving back and forth over the rugged landscape.

Rebecca ducked away as if she were afraid she would be seen. She scanned the cabin quickly, but there was nowhere to hide and she didn't think that heading out into the unknown, even with the shotgun, was a good idea.

She peeked again. The vehicle was definitely making its way in the direction of the cabin, albeit in what looked a haphazard manner, but that was probably because there was no road or track this far out and it was just a case of trying to navigate through the rocks and boulders.

Maybe it was Marshall? Maybe Gaby had changed her mind and sent her husband to come and get them? It didn't seem likely, but it was the least scary of the possible options.

Surely she hadn't been tracked here?

The thought trailed off in her mind as she knew there was only one way they could have found out where she was — by getting the information out of Will, and he wouldn't give that up without a fight.

Even the thought of it made all the colour drain from her face and her knees go weak. She slid down the wall to the ground and tried to take deep breaths.

Jack was at her side in an instant, licking her face, and somehow it made her think.

She couldn't just sit here — she had to do something! She had no idea what, but her mind tracked across the cabin to the shotgun which was resting in brackets on the wall.

With an effort she managed to get to her feet and cross the room. Her hands were shaking when she picked up the gun. She hadn't imagine that she could ever use it, but now, when she was faced with people who were coming to take her away against her will, maybe she could, to protect herself and her baby.

She broke the gun and checked it was loaded, even though she knew it was — she had watched Will do it. The thought of Will sent another wave of anguish through her and she had to put a hand out to steady herself.

There would be time to grieve later, but now she needed to focus on her baby. That would be what Will would have wanted. She shook her head at the idea of speaking of Will in the past tense. She knew nothing yet; she couldn't afford to let her imagination run down that route. For all she knew, it was Marshall — or maybe Will had made his way back early.

Both options seemed unlikely, but somehow the idea that all might not be lost was enough to get her feet moving.

She leaned against the wall by the window and tried to take a deep breath. Jack was like her shadow, at her side and ready. For what? Neither of them knew.

Rebecca leaned forward so she could take a quick peek out of the window. Was it her imagination, or had the pinpricks of light stopped moving? She risked another look and now she was sure. It was hard to tell in the dark how far away the vehicle was but its lights were still on. That seemed a strange approach for people who were presumably experienced in sneaking up on their target.

* * *

Rebecca had been watching the car for ten minutes. The headlights remained on and stationary but there was no movement from the car. Were they trying to draw her out? Rebecca couldn't be sure.

Jack had moved from her side and was standing by the door. Should she risk letting him out? Would that draw out whoever was in the car? She didn't want anything to happen to him but she was also sure that she couldn't stand there all night and just wait for something to happen. The pressure of just waiting was starting to build up and the greater it got the less able she felt to deal with whatever happened next.

Jack whined as she cracked open the door.

There was no movement from the car. She had no idea what game they were playing. With the shotgun under one arm and the torch in the other she stepped outside.

With only the two pinpoint lights of the car, she could make out no more than shadows. It was pitch dark, with the moon remaining hidden, and her torch beam didn't stretch far enough to illuminate the car.

Jack had his head tilted upwards as he sniffed the air and then he bounded forward. Rebecca tried to call him back but he seemed set on his path. This was exactly what she hadn't wanted. She didn't want Jack to try and defend her, she knew that wouldn't end well for him, and so she staggered forward, as close to running as she could get.

Jack was jumping up and down and barking, although the noise seemed to disperse on the wind. As Rebecca neared the car, her breath coming in short sharp gasps, she could see only one shadow in the car. One person.

Jack's barks were getting more frantic and Rebecca shone the torch in through the car windscreen — and then she could see why.

She dropped the shotgun and yanked open the door. Will crumpled out on to the ground.

Jack whined and started to lick Will's face. Rebecca shone the torch on him and could see that he was pale and his eyes were closed. She thought her heart would stop altogether as she dropped to her knees. Jack continued to whine as Rebecca reached out an unsteady hand.

'Will?' she said as her hand reached toward his chest. She shook him gently but he made no sign that he was aware she was there.

Rebecca swallowed the lump of fear in her throat and forced herself to think. He must be injured or sick. She used the torch to check his head. She could see no signs of injury, no bleeding or lumps. She worked her way down. His chest seemed fine but it was when she got to his right leg that she jolted with fright.

Someone, possibly Will, had tied a strip of shirt around his leg mid thigh, but this had been little help in stopping the bleeding.

With an instinct that she didn't know she possessed Rebecca placed a hand over the wound and pressed down hard. With her other hand she put down the torch and ran her hand around the back of Will's leg. She could find no obvious wound here but she had no idea if this was a good thing or a bad thing.

Her first aid at work course hadn't covered gunshot wounds! They weren't exactly common in an office environment. But she knew enough to know that she needed to stop the bleeding. She pressed down harder as she felt the warmth spread beneath her hand and this at last, got a response from Will, even if it was just a low groan. Rebecca could feel tears of relief run down her cheeks.

'Will?' she said softly, probably too softly for him to hear. 'Will!' She shouted this time, doubting that there was anyone else out there who could hear them.

She raised her free hand to his cheek, which felt cool and damp with sweat. She needed to get him back to the cabin. The problem was, she had no idea how to do that. What she needed was for Will to come round. She pressed harder on his wound, feeling guilty at the pain she was inflicting but hoping it would be enough.

Will's eyes flew open and he shot up into a seated position. Rebecca was so surprised by the sudden movement that she fell backwards with a small shriek. Will seemed to quickly take in where he was and what was happening — pretty impressive for someone who had only just regained consciousness.

'Are you OK?' Will asked and his look of concern almost made Rebecca laugh. Why was he worrying about her? She was in one piece, but the same could not be said for him.

'Me? *You're* the one who's been shot.'

Will glanced down at his leg as if he had just remembered.

'We need to get you back to the cabin,' Rebecca said, getting back onto her knees. 'Do you think you can stand long enough to get in the other side of the car?'

Will nodded as Rebecca got to her feet and held out a hand to him. He stared at it for a second as if he wasn't sure what to make of it. He tried to lever himself up but he seemed to quickly realise that he would need help, so he reached out for Rebecca's hand.

It took them three goes but she managed to get him upright, albeit swaying and with a fresh sheen of sweat across his face. She swung his arm over her shoulder and this time he didn't protest as she dragged him to the passenger seat. Will moaned in pain when Rebecca had to bend his injured leg to get it into the car but he made no complaint.

She closed the door and waited for Jack to jump in before squeezing herself behind the wheel.

Rebecca only had to drive a short distance but it seemed to take forever as her mind raced. Maybe she should turn the car around and try and make for Marshall's place, or see if she could find the road? Will needed medical attention urgently.

She slowed the car to a stop and Will opened his eyes.

'What are you doing?'

'You need a hospital,' Rebecca said.

'We have everything we need in the cabin,' Will said shaking his head but closing his eyes.

'I don't think a first aid kit is going to cover it and besides, I'm not a doctor.'

'Rangers are medics and Marshall gave us a full med kit. I can fix myself up.'

Rebecca looked at him doubtfully.

'We need to stay hidden.' His voice sounded as if the words were an effort to say. 'Please.'

Rebecca didn't reply, simply put the car back in gear and covered the short distance to the cabin. Was it selfish to do as he said? His priority seemed to be her, when surely now it was her turn to make sacrifices for him.

'I'll be fine, just give me a hand,' Will said as he pushed his door open. He seemed to have forgotten that Rebecca could only move so fast, particularly when she was trying to squeeze herself out from behind a steering wheel

— either that or he was just desperate to lie down.

Rebecca figured it was the latter so moved as fast as she was able — but not quick enough to prevent Will falling, but at least he only made it to one knee, his injured leg kicked out sideways.

Rebecca got an arm under his and braced herself as she hauled him to his feet. They both wobbled as she fought to keep her balance but Will reached out a hand to the roof of the car at the last minute and they managed to stay upright.

Rebecca shifted so that she could support some of his weight and they managed to lurch their way up the steps of the cabin and indoors. Jack raced over to the bed and sat waiting as Rebecca half-carried, half-dragged Will. She turned and dumped them both on the bed. For a few seconds she lay there, panting with the effort, and could feel Will doing the same.

As soon as she could, she got herself upright and then as gently as possible lifted Will's legs on to the bed. He was at a funny angle but at least he was lying down.

Rebecca had left two hurricane lamps on hooks each side of the bed and so for the first time she was able to see Will properly. He did not look good. His face was pale and dark circles surrounded his eyes. His hair was damp with sweat and his face was creased in pain.

Rebecca wasn't sure what she was supposed to do first so grabbed a blanket and threw it over Will's chest. She remembered that it was important to keep a patient warm, but other than that her mind felt blank.

'Grab the med kit, it's in the box by the door,' Will said, eyes closed, his voice sounding croaky.

Rebecca hurried over to the box and pulled it open. Will hadn't been exaggerating, the box seemed to contain a mini hospital! She tried to pick it up but it felt heavy, so instead she used her foot to push it across the floor to the bed.

'We need to clean the wound and find the bullet,' Will said.

Rebecca stared, wondering if it was her imagination or had he just said 'we'?

'Right,' she said, giving herself a shake. Now was not the time to be squeamish. After everything Will had done for her, she was going to help him now even if the thought of it sent a wave of nausea through her stomach.

'The bottle of pink stuff is antiseptic. Pour it in the metal tray.'

Rebecca pulled a tin tray in the shape of a kidney and placed it on the bed before tipping some of the pink liquid in. It had a strong smell and she winced, as she knew it would cause Will burning pain.

'Grab some gloves and put them on, then open a pack of swabs. You need to soak them in the antiseptic and wash out the wound.'

Like most people, Rebecca had never tried to put on a set of surgical gloves and it wasn't easy. Her hands were sweating and the gloves seemed to stick to all the wrong parts of her hands. Eventually she managed to wrestle them on enough that she could use most of her fingers. Getting in to the sealed pack of swabs was even more difficult.

'Use your teeth,' Will said sounding as if he were gritting his.

Rebecca tore at the pack with her teeth and released the swabs, before soaking them in the pink liquid. Will had leaned forward to pull off his temporary dressing and the effort brought a fresh wave of pain and sweat.

Rebecca pressed him back down on the bed.

'This is going to hurt,' she said, somewhat unnecessarily. Will just nodded, but she saw that he grabbed a handful of blanket in one fist.

Gently she wiped at the edges of the wound.

'Not a time to be gentle. You've got to get right in there and clean it up.'

Rebecca could feel her hands shake as she tried to do as she was asked.

'I can do it,' he said with a gasp, but now it was Rebecca's turn to shake her head. She squeezed the swab and a trickle of antiseptic went into the small hole the bullet had made. Will jerked.

'That's it,' he said. 'Now you need to get the surgical pack. It's wrapped in plastic about the size of a paperback.'

Rebecca found it and placed it on the bed.

'Take off your gloves and unwrap it. There's a set of sterile gloves. Put them on and then use the forceps to retrieve the bullet.'

Rebecca's ears rang with the words but she did as she was told and managed to unwrap the pack before pulling on a fresh pair of gloves. She picked up the set of forceps and looked anxiously at the wound.

'You have to do this. The bullet will cause infection, if it hasn't already.'

Will was panting with the effort of speaking and Rebecca knew he wouldn't be able to get the bullet out himself. As delicately as she could she pushed the ends of the forceps into the wound. Will managed to stay still and it was only a quick glance at his face that told Rebecca how much pain she was inflicting.

She thought she felt something beneath the tip of the forceps and pulled back but there was no bullet.

'S'OK. Try again,' Will said, his fists turning white as he gripped the blanket.

Rebecca forced herself to take a deep breath and focus. She needed to do this and she needed to get it done now. Again she tried, and finally, on the third attempt, she pulled back to find the small bullet, now mushroom-shaped from the impact, attached to the end of her forceps.

'Great job. Clean the wound again. Pack it with fresh gauze to stop the bleeding. Then dress it.'

Rebecca didn't answer, just focused on doing what she had been told. It wasn't the best-looking bandage she had ever seen but at least the wound was now clean and covered.

'I'm all done,' she said but looking at

Will's face she saw that he had either passed out or fallen asleep. She was only surprised that he managed to stay with her for as long as he had.

She pulled the blanket over his legs before going to the fire and loading it up with more wood.

She took a bottle of water from one of the boxes and then carried one of the chairs so that she could sit at Will's side and keep watch. All she could do now was wait and hope that her novice attempts at surgery had been enough.

15

Rebecca had tried not to become obsessed with the passing of time. After everything Will had been through she knew she shouldn't be surprised if he slept for hours, but still, with every passing minute she felt her anxiety rise.

Should she go for help? She didn't want to leave him by himself and even if she did manage to navigate her way back to the homestead, what if something happened while she was away?

The sun was starting to rise and light was filtering through the windows. The chairs were not designed to be sat on for hours by pregnant women and so Rebecca had been walking up and down the open plan room. Anything to ease the pain in her back and to keep her awake.

Jack looked up at her from time to time but seemed content to stay where he was, at Will's side. He at least seemed to have managed to get some sleep, judging by the snores coming from his side of the bed. Rebecca's belly made a loud grumbling noise and Jack looked up, his head cocked, and ears pricked up.

'You hungry too?' Rebecca asked softly.

Jack whined, which she took as a yes, so she opened a new can of dog food and filled his bowl. Jack had wolfed up the contents before Rebecca could start on anything for herself and he looked up at her expectantly.

'You can forget that,' she told him. 'We're out of eggs and bacon.'

'I brought supplies. They're in the car,' Will's voice said from the bed.

Rebecca rushed over but Jack still managed to beat her to it. He jumped on the bed and started to lick Will's face, which now had the shadow of beard growth but his colour was slightly better. Rebecca perched on the chair beside the bed.

'How are you feeling?'

'How long have I been asleep?' Will asked, pulling himself so that he was sitting up and reached down to brace his leg.

'About ten hours.'

Rebecca knew exactly how long it had been, since she had been mentally recording the minutes that had gone past, but she didn't think it would be sensible to tell Will that.

Will nodded and wiped at his lips. Rebecca handed him the water bottle that she had left by the bed in preparation for this moment and watched as he drank half of it down in one go.

'I'll get you something to eat,' Rebecca said, making to stand up.

'In a minute. I'm sure you want to know what progress I made with the plan.'

Rebecca gave him a look. 'I guess I sort of assumed that you hadn't made it that far.'

'You've under estimated me, Miss Buckingham,' Will said and a smile tugged at his lips. It was such a relief to hear him making a joke that she laughed out loud.

'I would never do that, Sheriff,' she said in a similar tone.

'Good. We Rangers can get a bit precious about things like that.' Will returned her smile and then winced as his leg seemed to spasm.

'Here,' Rebecca said handing him a small brown glass bottle.

'I need to stay alert,' he said.

'Fine,' Rebecca said not bothering to keep her crossness from her voice. 'At least take some of these.' She handed him a blister pack of Tylenol. They wouldn't make him sleepy, so he had no excuse. Will swallowed down a couple.

'And now these,' Rebecca said handing him two capsules of antibiotics. She raised an eyebrow, daring him to argue but he didn't, just swallowed them down.

'I probably should take a look at your wound,' Rebecca said although if she was honest she wasn't sure what warning signs she should be looking out for.

Presumably Will had enough experience to know whether it was healing or not.

The problem was, she thought, she wasn't sure if he would tell her if it looked bad. If he did, she would insist that they needed to get him to a hospital and she knew he would refuse. Whatever had happened to him, Will seemed to think they were safer here than anywhere else.

'That can wait,' Will said and patted the bed beside him.

Rebecca stayed where she was. Her back was screaming at her to lie down and now that Will was awake, her anxiety had lessened enough for the tiredness to break through.

'I won't bite and I'm guessing you've been sitting in that chair all night.'

Rebecca knew when she had been backed into a corner. If she made a fuss now she would only succeed in embarrassing herself, so she walked around the bed as Will arranged some pillows for her and she lay back, propped up, and tried not to let the relief show.

Her limbs felt heavy and she was sure if she just closed her eyes she would sleep. But she needed to know what had happened and that overruled any physical need for sleep.

Jack snuggled into the gap between them and was soon snoring — apparently he wasn't worried what had happened but was just happy that they were both back and safe.

'So?' Rebecca said as Will took a sip from his water bottle.

'I made it to my meet and I was able to convince my contact to look into the situation. On my way back I was spotted. One of them managed to get away a lucky shot, but I made it to the car and lost them en route.'

Rebecca raised an eyebrow to indicate that she wasn't impressed with his minimal storytelling style.

'My contact works for the FBI. I explained who I thought was after you and that was enough to pique her interest.'

'She was interested in the Barter

family?' Rebecca wanted to know more about Will's contact. How did he know her? But she stopped her imagination in its tracks. Will needed to rest and so did she. She needed to let Will tell her the relevant details and then she would make them some food and they could both rest.

'No, their reach hasn't got as far as the US.'

'Then who?' Rebecca asked the question as her brain started to make the connection. Something about the people who had visited her grandad's cabin had been enough to convince Will to run for it. She could have smacked herself for not putting the pieces together sooner. Will shifted and Rebecca knew that he had kept information from her.

'Why didn't you tell me you recognised them?'

She shifted so she could see his face. He was good at hiding his feelings but she felt she was getting to know him now and maybe she could see something there. She wanted the truth.

'I figured you already knew enough about the Barter family to be afraid. I didn't feel it would be helpful.' He turned his gaze from straight ahead to look at her. Apparently, her expression was easy to read.

'It's my life,' she said softly, 'and I have a right to know.'

'I'm sorry. I should have told you. I recognised one of the gang. He only works for a few of the untouchable crime families. He brings the game the Barter family are playing to a whole new level. He's a ruthless enforcer whose reputation is well known in crime fighting agencies.'

Rebecca leaned back on her pillows. She would never tell Will but she was almost glad that he hadn't told her until now. He was right, she had already been scared and hadn't needed any more information to know that she needed to run as fast and as far away as she could.

Her hand went instinctively to her belly as she felt again the need to protect her baby from its father's family. Whatever happened, she would keep her baby safe.

'It may not seem like it, but actually that's the first piece of good news we've had.'

Rebecca frowned as she tried to figure out how on earth a leading enforcer could be good news. All she could see was how determined James's father was to bring her back to the family, and she shivered at the thought. She looked down as Will picked up her hand and held it.

'It means that we have a lot of resources going after him now. The man is like a ghost and his actions are difficult to predict, but . . .' Will didn't finish his sentence, he didn't really need to.

'But now they may be able to predict where he might be?'

Will squeezed her hand. 'It's a real opportunity to track him. Usually we only know where he's been but now we know his target.'

Rebecca swallowed the lump in her throat. Being a target was not a comforting thought.

'Rebecca, he may be an enforcer, but his job would be to ensure no harm comes to you and the baby. That's the only way he would get paid. His reputation is for getting the job done, whatever it might be. That's the only reason I agreed to come back here and stay. He won't risk a frontal assault — it would be too dangerous.'

Rebecca looked down at Will's leg. The enforcer might not be willing to risk *her* life, but he certainly had no qualms when it came to Will.

'Was he the one who shot you?'

'It was hard to tell. I was too busy trying to make it to my car, but I suspect he was there, even if he didn't make the shot.'

'So we wait here until he comes?'

'We wait here and hope the FBI get him first. There aren't too many places to hide out here.'

'What about Marshall and Gaby?' Rebecca said, sitting up suddenly.

'They're covered. The FBI have units

watching the road. I doubt the enforcer would risk coming in that way. We think he'll try and come through the National Park — much easier to come under the radar that way.'

'Are you sure they'll be OK? I couldn't bear to bring them any more trouble.'

'The FBI are going to make contact and offer to move them but they don't believe it's necessary.'

Rebecca sighed. Without meaning to they had dragged Marshall and his family into her mess.

'It was the best we could do, we involved them as soon as I decided to come here.'

Will looked tortured by his decision. Now it was Rebecca's turn to squeeze his hand. If only she had managed to get away then she wouldn't have drawn Will into her mess. Then she wouldn't have indirectly forced him to put his own friends at risk. But in truth she doubted she would still be free without him, and the thought of being taken back to the Barters set off a fresh wave of fear.

'Stop,' Will said. It was a command. Rebecca looked at him. 'I know what you're thinking and you need to stop. This is not your fault.'

'Well, it's not your fault either,' Rebecca said.

'You're right. We can't focus on that, we need to focus on what's happening now.'

Rebecca had to fight the urge to dissolve into his arms. There was nothing she wanted more in that moment than to be held by someone who must care on some level, surely. After everything he had done for her, he had to feel something.

Will released her hand and Rebecca could feel the imprint of his hand in hers, and she felt as if a part of her was missing. As Will slid his arm around her shoulder, she wondered if she was dreaming, perhaps she had fallen asleep? But it felt too real and too good to be a dream. Tentatively she leaned into him and he shifted so that she could lie comfortably in his arms.

With her head tucked under Will's chin, Rebecca thought she would be happy to stay there forever.

'Is this what you meant by focusing on right now?' She raised a hand to cover her mouth when she realised she had said the words out loud. She felt Will's chest rumble beneath her as he laughed, and she giggled too.

'I should be focusing on the issues at hand, but I found I couldn't resist any longer. All I could think about on the drive back was that I had to get to you. I had to keep my promise to you.'

'And you did — although I'm not sure a gunshot wound to your leg counts as being in one piece.'

'I'm a Ranger, we don't count the scratches.'

'A gunshot wound is a scratch?'

'More of an inconvenience.'

Rebecca elbowed him gently but he made a show of being injured.

'Hey! I've been shot, remember?'

'I thought it was just an inconvenience?'

'I may have over-exaggerated my manliness.'

'I don't think that's possible.'

This time Rebecca's eyes went wide. What was she thinking — and more importantly what was she saying? It was as if the filter between her brain and her mouth was fried. She kept saying things out loud that should remain in her head.

'It's always nice to be appreciated,' Will murmured softly.

Rebecca twisted her head and planted a soft kiss on his cheek.

'Thank you,' she said. 'It's not enough, I know, but I don't know what else to say.'

Rebecca hadn't moved her face away and she could feel Will studying her. She watched as a battle raged, not on his face but in the depths of his eyes. Then there was something else — a decision, perhaps?

Whatever it was, he leaned down and kissed her back — not on the cheek but on the lips. As his lips brushed hers, she lifted up a hand to cradle his head and their kiss deepened as she responded in kind.

It was Jack's bark that broke them apart.

Will went from being lost in the kiss to full alert in a heartbeat. He leaned forward as if he wanted to protect Rebecca with his body.

Jack was sitting in front of them with his head on one side, as if he was trying to work out what they were doing. Then he whined before burrowing into the almost non-existent gap between them.

'I think Jack is jealous,' Rebecca said softly as she reached out and ruffled the dog's ears.

'I would be jealous too, if I was him,' Will said as he leaned in for another kiss. 'But he's also right — we can't stay in bed all day.'

He didn't add the word 'kissing' but Rebecca could tell it was there. The air between them seemed charged.

'As much as we might want to.' His voice was husky and Rebecca felt a shiver run through her that had nothing to do with fear.

She knew he was right and that she needed space to think. Before the kiss, the idea of being with Will had been a fantasy, something that had helped her cope with the loneliness and sense of loss. She had left James, but she felt she had lost him the moment he had told her the truth about his family and what he actually did for a living. Was she just fixating on the first man she came across, a man who had helped her beyond what she could have expected?

It seemed that Will felt something too, but was that just a confusion of emotions at the mess they found themselves in? How would he feel when it was over? If it ever was.

'I'll make us some food. You must be hungry,' Rebecca said, shifting to widen the space between them, sure that she would need to move away in stages or her heart would take over again.

'I can make us something,' Will said and made to swing his legs out of bed.

Rebecca stopped him with a hand on his arm. 'No! You need to rest.'

'So do you,' Will said and his eyes slid once more to her pregnant belly. Rebecca wasn't sure what she read there. Could he imagine bringing up another man's child? She shook the thoughts away. She needed to focus on the here and now.

She wondered if it was safe for them both to be asleep at the same time. Was this one of those situations where one of you should be on the alert? Rebecca figured it probably qualified but she wasn't sure if she could keep her eyes open if she lay down, even with the threats that surrounded them — she was beyond tired.

'You make the food and then sleep. I'll take the first watch,' Will suggested.

Rebecca thought about arguing but knew Will was right. Not that she was sure what either of them would do if the enforcer arrived.

She walked to the door and opened it, Jack jumped off the bed and was by her side in an instant. Rebecca reached down and scratched his head.

'I'm just going to go out and get the supplies,' she said to the dog as if he needed the reassurance, but somehow, she couldn't get her feet to move. She knew the feeling of safety that she had being inside the cabin was artificial but still it seemed like a haven.

'I can go,' Will said from behind her and before she could react he had slid his legs off the bed and was doing his best to stand.

Rebecca rushed to his side and gently pushed him back to a sitting position.

'Don't be ridiculous. I parked the car outside, it's a two-minute job, tops.'

She could feel Will look at her and knew that he understood her fears.

'Do you think I should move the car round the back — hide it?' Rebecca said, feeling the need to try and shift the conversation to something other than her own fear.

'I expect they have resources that means they could see the car from the air.'

'Helicopter?'

Rebecca hadn't even thought that was a possibility. People in her circles back home didn't have access to things like that. Taxis maybe — but helicopters, no. Not for the first time she felt as if she had accidentally wandered on to the set of an action movie.

'They'll easily be able to find us, then,' Rebecca said bleakly, circling her bump and feeling her breath go ragged.

Will managed to get himself to his feet and pulled her into an unsteady hug.

'The FBI will be able to track them if they do, I promise,' he said.

'I thought in the movies people were offered safe houses,' Rebecca murmured into his shoulder. She had always wondered at the fact that houses seemed to mysteriously appear and be available just when the hero needed them.

'They do — but not when they want to catch people,' he said.

Rebecca pulled away a little but held on to Will's arms. She wasn't sure he would be able to stay upright without her support.

'Are we bait?'

She wasn't sure which sensation was going to win over — anger at the risks they were taking, or impressed at the audacity of the plan. She couldn't believe the thought hadn't occurred to her before now.

'More of a lure. If we went into hiding they would likely never track them down.'

Rebecca couldn't think about this. All she could think about was the fact that she was heavily pregnant and in a cabin in the middle of nowhere hoping that the FBI would arrive before the bad guys did.

How could Will think this was a good plan?

'It's the only way for you and the baby to be safe in the long term.'

'That's funny because right now I feel like we're in more danger than we've ever been.'

'The enforcer will never risk hurting

you, Rebecca. He won't get his money that way. Besides, I doubt he wants the wrath of the Barter family in his life.'

'He might not hurt me but he has no qualms about hurting you.' She gestured at his leg. It was bad enough if they were both at risk but if Will was the only one risking his life, she didn't think she could bear it. Assuming that she believed the premise that the enforcer would never risk her being hurt.

'I know I'm asking a lot, but I need you to trust me. If there was any other way I thought we could resolve this I would take it, believe me.'

It was all too much to process.

Rebecca gently disentangled herself from Will. She was afraid for herself and for the baby and for Will but at the same time a small part of her brain told her that Will was right. This might be their only chance to end this. If they ran, they would be running forever — and what kind of life would that be for her child?

'I don't like it,' Rebecca said.

Will opened his mouth to argue but Rebecca held up her hand.

'But yes, I think you might be right. I have no idea how my life has come to this but . . . ' She closed her eyes and tried to take a slow, deep breath. 'You need to promise me one thing.'

'Anything.'

'Promise me you won't put yourself in harm's way,' she said.

He raised an eyebrow.

'That's kind of an occupational hazard.'

Rebecca was not to be distracted by his attempt at levity.

'Will . . . ' she started to say.

'OK, OK, I promise I will only do what is necessary to keep you and the baby safe.'

Rebecca knew that was the only promise she could expect him to make.

She wanted him to promise to protect himself but she knew he would never do that. Even if he had no feelings for her, it was ingrained in him to protect others.

It was as natural to Will as breathing, she understood that now.

She made a silent promise to herself that she would do whatever she could to ensure that Will was safe too — but there was no need to share that thought with him.

16

They had eaten and then Will had insisted that Rebecca lie down and get some sleep. She protested, too afraid that something might happen while she slept, but she was lost in moments, her body's need to rest overriding any other desires.

The first thing she knew was a hand on her shoulder, shaking her firmly. Rebecca's eyes flew open and she sat bolt upright, ready to do what, she wasn't sure. She wasn't exactly in a condition to fight but she also knew she would do what she had to.

She felt a hand cover her mouth and tried to pull away. Then her eyes focused on Will. He held a finger to his lips and she nodded to show that she understood.

It was dark in the one-roomed cabin. Will had either not lit the lanterns or had snuffed them out. In his hand he held a small torch.

'What is it?' Rebecca whispered.

Then she heard it and the sound answered her own question. Will's guess had been right. Overhead the sound of blades chopping through the night air could be heard. The sound seemed to fade in and then out again.

'They're doing a quadrant search.'

Rebecca didn't need to ask who the 'they' were. She doubted Will would have reacted in this way if he thought it was the FBI. Rebecca looked up at the ceiling — silly she knew, it wasn't like she could see anything from in here.

'Do you think they've found us?' she whispered urgently as the helicopter noise faded out again.

'Yes,' Will said, his voice curt. Rebecca knew he was just focused on the mission but his tone cut through her all the same.

'What should we do?'

She allowed the fear of discovery to push away the pain. Will turned to her, his face lit up with the dim light of the pen torch and she could see a merciless glint in his eye.

'We wait. I left a few surprises for them.'

Suddenly there was the sound of fireworks, popping and cracking.

Rebecca looked to Will who shrugged and offered her his hand. She managed to get herself to the edge of the bed and he pulled her to her feet. Following him in the dark, it looked as if Will had built a mini fort. All the furniture had been shifted to create various barriers.

There was a blanket folded on the floor and Will gestured for her to sit on it. Jack was quickly at her side and Rebecca got the distinct impression he had been given his orders to protect her.

Will held up his hand and she wasn't sure whether he was commanding Jack to stay or her. Jack whined but stayed beside her, leaning in so she could feel his warmth.

Will turned away and took the light with him.

'Stay down until I tell you otherwise.'

'Where are the FBI?' Rebecca said, suddenly overwhelmed with panic that they had been left alone, deserted by any help, and that Will would be taking on their enemy by himself even though he'd had no time to recover from his injuries.

'They'll be on their way,' Will's voice cut through the darkness. 'They know it's started. My greeting will have told them that.'

Rebecca now understood that the fireworks weren't just to warn them that the enemy was at their door but to send the same message to the FBI. She could only hope they were close enough to help before the fight was over.

She wasn't so much frightened for herself. Now that she had time to think about it, Will's words made sense. Whoever had come for her would not want to risk hurting her, or at least the baby, so she was safe from the assault, even if not for the long term future. But the enforcer had shown no such qualms about Will — and she couldn't let him pay for her mistakes.

Jack barked as she got on to her hands and knees and started to crawl out of the protective fort that Will had built for her. She ignored Jack but kept her head down and made her way in the direction of the door. There was light outside now and some of it spilled through the gap in the door. She could hear shouting, too indistinct to make out the words, but she could hear enough to know that it wasn't Will.

She had to help him. If she appeared by his side, surely the enforcer would call off his men. Then maybe, just maybe, the FBI would arrive before the enforcer could take her away.

It was a risk she had to take because she couldn't let Will be injured again — or worse. She couldn't let her mind think about what the worse might be and crawled on towards the door.

She yanked open the door with one hand and ducked down with her back against the wall. She could hear the rat-tat-tat sound of gunfire. It was overwhelming and she couldn't tell what direction it was coming from. As the door swung back on its hinges, she heard more shouting. One voice in particular seemed to be close by and it sounded furious.

Lying half on her belly she started to shout as she crawled on to the front step. 'Stop!'

She screeched as loud as she could but was doubtful that her words could be heard.

There was a flurry of fur as Jack placed himself in front of her, his hackles up. She would only be able to move forward now if she pushed him out of the way but she had no intention of moving.

Bright spotlights ripped through the darkness and she was sure the enforcer had spotted her.

For a brief moment there was silence and then a single pop. The air was filled with smoke that burned her eyes and tasted bitter.

Jack barked and Rebecca pulled him down beside her. It seemed time stood still. The smoke reached her lungs and she coughed as her eyes ran. She wanted to wriggle back into the cabin and slam the door, but couldn't move.

All around her was noise of booted feet and shouts and she knew the safest thing she could do was stay as still as possible and keep her head down. She could only hope she had done enough to keep Will safe.

Please let him be safe, she prayed.

Rebecca felt like she had been there for hours but knew it was more likely seconds, maybe not even a minute.

'Ms Buckingham.'

The voice wasn't Will. Rebecca didn't know what to do but looked up to see a figure, dressed from head to toe in black leaning over her. She had no idea if this person was friend or foe.

'Ms Buckingham? I'm Agent Creely.'

The figure pulled off the black balaclava to reveal a woman of about the same age as her.

'FBI,' she said, although it probably didn't need saying at this point. 'You're safe now, ma'am. Let me help you up.'

A surprisingly gentle hand reached for Rebecca's arm and she was soon sitting upright, her back leaning against the wall, Jack's head on her lap. Jack sniffed suspiciously at Agent Creely but then licked her hand and the woman smiled.

Rebecca's brain seemed to be kicking into action and she started to form a picture of what had just happened.

'Will!' she screamed, desperately trying to get to her feet. The hands were back, keeping her where she was.

'We have him. He's on the air flight to hospital. He's injured and in need of medical treatment. He's been shot.'

Rebecca could feel the darkness flood in around her. Her vision narrowed, and air rushed in her ears. She dimly heard a shout and Jack whining and then nothing.

★   ★   ★

When Rebecca woke, she was lying on her side with blankets over her. She felt comfortable and safe, even though she had no idea where she was.

There was beeping in the background and she wondered if she had set an alarm clock, so she opened her eyes to look.

She was in a hospital room, surrounded by monitors. A nurse sat on a chair at the end of the bed but when she saw that Rebecca was awake she stood up with a smile.

'Miss Buckingham, welcome back.'

The nurse moved the table nearer to Rebecca and poured her a glass of water. Rebecca lifted her hand to pick it up and realised that she had an IV tube running in to her arm. She frowned at it, thinking it was unnecessary. 'Where's Will?'

'He's just out of surgery and awake. He's doing just fine,' the nurse said reassuringly.

'I have to go and see him,' Rebecca said throwing back the covers and sliding her feet to the floor. Just as she was about to stand up, a wave of pain seemed to tighten around her middle like a vice. She gasped.

'What . . . ?' was the only word she could squeeze out through her gritted teeth.

'Miss Buckingham.'

'Rebecca,' she hissed.

'Rebecca . . . you are in labour.'

'No, I'm not,' Rebecca said, straightening up as the pain vanished as quickly as it came. 'I'm not due for another few weeks.'

'Well, your baby has other ideas and quite frankly after what you've been through, I'm surprised the little one has waited this long.'

'Is the baby OK?' Rebecca asked, cradling her stomach protectively.

'Baby's just fine and coping with the contractions well. Right now you need to focus on you and your child. I've asked a friend on surgical to keep me apprised of your partner's progress.'

Rebecca thought about correcting

the misunderstanding but if the nurse hadn't meant partner as in romantic partner then the conversation would get embarrassing fast, so she let it go. She took a sip of water.

'I'll get you something to eat. You'll need to keep up your strength,' the nurse said. 'Buzz if you need anything before I get back.' The nurse gestured at the call bell that was on the table and Rebecca nodded.

There was so much to take in. She was having her baby today and Will was OK, but what about the Barter family? At first she thought the pain was from thinking of them, but she quickly realised it was another contraction.

The door opened and the nurse returned, carrying a plate of sandwiches.

'Another contraction?' the nurse asked, placing the sandwiches on the table and turning to check the monitor. 'You'll be moving into the final stage before you know it.'

The nurse smiled as if this was a good thing. Rebecca suspected it was;

she wasn't sure how long she could do this for. Right now the pain was overwhelming any other thoughts.

Then again it passed and she panted in relief.

'Try and eat something before the next one comes,' the nurse said.

Rebecca didn't feel hungry but thought the nurse might be right and picked up a sandwich.

'Do you know where my dog is?' she asked after she swallowed a bite.

'The FBI lady is looking after him. He's been quite a hit with them, I believe. She said he can stay with her until you're ready to have him back.'

Rebecca nodded. 'Do you know what happened with the . . . ' Rebecca wasn't sure how to explain what had happened at the cabin.

'I don't know the details, but the good guys came out on top. Agent Creely wanted to come and discuss it with you but I've said it can wait until after . . . '

Rebecca opened her mouth to argue

but no words came as the pain returned again.

★ ★ ★

Four hours later, Rebecca had no idea which way was up. She had refused pain relief which she was starting to think had been a foolish idea. She didn't want to be paralysed, albeit temporarily. What if she needed to run with the baby? She knew she was probably being irrational but she couldn't shake the thought and so had turned down every offer of something to help.

All she wanted was Will, but he was recovering and besides, she hadn't figured out what was going on between them — a first date with her giving birth didn't seem like a good plan!

The nurse said matter of factly, 'Time to push.'

Rebecca had no idea what time it was. She had been pushing and following instructions but she was lost in a fog of pain and confusion.

All she could think about was that she was alone, despite the fact that the room had been filling with people with increasingly concerned looks on their faces.

She could hear someone calling out a name and it sounded like Will. Rebecca couldn't imagine who would be shouting for him and then realised that it was probably her. She knew Will wouldn't come, he couldn't, even if he wanted to, and she had no idea if he would want to anyway. Her mind swirled with the thought as a fresh wave of pain hit her hard.

Something was wrong. She just knew something was wrong. Something was wrong with the baby and she was all alone.

'The baby?' she managed to gasp.

She couldn't form any more words but the face that appeared in front of her appeared to be trying to tell her something. She shook her head trying to show that she didn't understand, that she couldn't hear.

She closed her eyes and prayed. *Please let the baby be all right.* She repeated the mantra over and over again. A hand gripped hers. Another hand brushed against her forehead.

Rebecca opened her eyes. Will was there!

He couldn't be of course, but somehow even a ghostly image of him was comforting and she wasn't about to complain that her pain-wracked brain had managed to conjure him up in her hour of need.

'Rebecca. The baby is distressed. They're going to take you to theatre.'

Rebecca gripped his imaginary hand. If she could just hold on to the dream then maybe, just maybe, everything would be all right.

'I'm here and I'll stay with you,' he said.

Rebecca smiled that her mind had managed to say all the right things.

She felt him lean closer.

'I'll always be here, Rebecca, as long as you want me.'

She frowned slightly at that and then it felt as if the room was moving.

Lights passed over her and she could hear noises and calm but terse voices.

Still-imaginary Will held her hand tightly.

The bed she was in crashed through a set of doors and then she felt her grip on Will's hand loosen and she knew she couldn't do it by herself and despite her fight, she gave in to the blackness.

17

Rebecca couldn't open her eyes. She was too tired and the effort seemed too much. She could hear muffled sounds and could feel that she was not alone, wherever she was.

As her brain started to register sensations she realised that someone was holding her hand. Somehow she knew it was Will, or at least her brain had been kind enough to let his imaginary image stay.

She turned her head as she heard a noise. She couldn't place it but she knew it was important. The grip on her hand tightened. She knew she had to see so she forced her eyes open. She caught a snap shot of the room before her eyelids slid closed again.

With a deep breath she forced herself to open them again. Standing next to her bed, for now she knew she was lying down, was a figure in scrubs holding something in her arms. All of a sudden Rebecca knew where she was, knew what the last thing she remembered was.

'My baby,' she croaked.

The hand squeezed her hand again. 'Your baby's fine, Rebecca.'

Rebecca frowned. She knew that voice but it couldn't be him. She turned her head in the direction and saw Will sitting in a wheelchair by her bed.

'Will?'

She was more confused now than ever but she couldn't keep her eyes away from the person in scrubs, the person who was holding a baby, tightly wrapped in blankets. Her baby? She felt so confused and it must have shown on her face.

'You had to have an emergency Caesarean but both you and the baby are doing well,' the kindly voice said. Rebecca recognised it as the nurse who had been with her before. 'Would you like to hold your baby?' the nurse asked.

Rebecca was trying to sit up. She winced with pain but ignored it and held out her arms. The nurse gently placed the bundle in Rebecca's arms and she saw the face of her child for the first time.

'Would you like to know if you have a boy or a girl?' the nurse asked and all Rebecca could do was nod, her throat and chest so tight with emotion that she knew she wouldn't be able to speak.

'You have a baby girl, Rebecca.' This time the voice was not the nurse's. 'Congratulations, she's beautiful,' Will said.

Rebecca couldn't take her eyes off of her daughter, the baby she had been longing to meet and had gone to such lengths to protect. She had a halo of soft, pale hair and a rosebud mouth, and long eyelashes that fluttered in her sleep.

'Hello,' she said softly, 'I'm your mummy.'

Just saying the words out loud brought tears to her eyes and Rebecca let them fall. A gentle hand wiped them away and then a soft kiss was placed on her forehead.

'You're really here,' she said.

'She certainly knows how to make an entrance,' Will agreed.

Rebecca tore her gaze away for a second to look at Will before turning her attention back to her baby.

'I meant you, Will.'

'I promised I would be.'

Rebecca frowned. 'You were with me before? I thought I had imagined it.'

'I was told you were calling out my name, so I wheeled myself down here.'

'Despite doctor's orders,' the nurse said dryly. 'And we haven't been able to get him to leave your side since.'

'I didn't want you to be alone,' Will said, leaning over a little so he could look at the baby too. 'Although I don't suppose you are any more.'

Rebecca caressed the soft layer of hair on her baby's head.

'Does she have a name?' the nurse asked, checking the monitors and making a note on the clipboard at the end of Rebecca's bed.

'No, not really. I had a few ideas but . . . ' Rebecca closed her eyes. She knew she couldn't share this moment with James, not if she and the baby wanted to be safe, but at the same time she felt sad that he couldn't see his daughter.

'You have time,' Will said.

Rebecca looked at him. His face seemed to register the battling emotions she was going through. Relief that the baby was here and safe, but also that she would likely never meet her biological father. Rebecca couldn't imagine a circumstance when that could happen. James had made his allegiances clear and she doubted he would ever want to see her again, particularly if Will's plan to bring down the Barter family succeeded.

'I'll leave you in peace. If you need anything just press the bell,' the nurse said and walked from the room, pulling the sliding patio-style door closed behind her.

'Are you OK?' Rebecca asked.

275

'Well, not that you didn't do a brilliant job in patching me up, but there was some muscle damage that needed fixing. I'll be back to normal in a few days.'

Rebecca raised an eyebrow but kept her gaze on her daughter. 'Agent Creely said you were hurt and I thought . . . ' Rebecca felt her throat close up once more with the overwhelming emotion.

'My leg started to bleed again and so they were keen to drag me off to the hospital. I didn't want to leave without you but I wasn't given much choice in the matter.'

Rebecca looked at him now. She couldn't imagine anyone could persuade him to do anything he didn't want to do.

'I may have passed out . . . ' Will said, colour outlining his cheeks and Rebecca smiled. That certainly made more sense from what she knew of him — and it also awoke the notion that maybe he had feelings for her, as she did for him. Only time would tell, she guessed, whether they both felt the same once the danger was over.

She tightened her grip on her daughter. 'Are we safe?' she whispered, her voice sounding hoarse to her own ears.

'For now, yes. The FBI have the enforcer and his crew in custody.'

'And the Barters?'

'We'll have to wait and see on that front but I promised you I would keep you safe — and I will.'

'You have a life to get back to.' Rebecca forced herself to say the words. She didn't want to but somehow she knew that knowing the truth now would be easier than waiting.

'That life can wait until you're safe.'

Rebecca nodded. That was probably all she could expect him to say at this point but somehow it made her heart sink. Maybe he was just staying with her until she was safe and then he would go home and she would have to figure out what she was going to do next — what she and the baby were going to do. That was assuming this would ever truly be over.

Rebecca felt a wave of cold and tiredness wash over her and she shivered.

'You need to rest,' Will said, concerned.

'I've only just woken up,' Rebecca said. She was so tired, but she didn't think she could bear to close her eyes now that her baby was finally in her arms.

'From anaesthetic after major surgery. It's not like you've had eight hours' proper rest.' Will's eyes flashed.

'I don't want to leave her,' Rebecca whispered softly as the baby caught hold of her finger.

'You won't be leaving her. She can sleep in her cot, right here next to you — and I'll stay with you both until you wake up.'

Rebecca looked at Will. Once more he had managed to read her mind. She didn't want to leave her baby alone.

'But you need to rest, too.'

Will flicked his eyes to a folded bed

that had been set up next to Rebecca's hospital bed.

'We can take it in turns. You rest for a few hours and then I'll have my turn.'

Rebecca placed a kiss on her daughter's forehead and she barely stirred. Will leaned across and lifted the baby expertly from her arms. He looked as if he had done that many times before.

Will saw her surprise and smiled, saying, 'I have six younger brothers and sisters. I've had plenty of practice — Peggy was the best teacher.'

Rebecca rested back on the pillows and closed her eyes, thinking how much she hoped that Peggy would get to meet the baby one day.

⋆　⋆　⋆

The sound of crying broke through Rebecca's dream. As she woke she couldn't remember the details but for the first time in a long while, she knew it had been a good dream, one where she had been happy and safe.

The crying settled into soft snuffles and Rebecca turned her head. Will had her baby in his arms and he was feeding her with a bottle. His eyes were soft, as if tears weren't too far away, and he was focused entirely on the baby. For her part, the baby was reaching up to hold the bottle and linked her tiny fingers around one of his. She was gazing up at him with such a look of trust that Rebecca felt dampness on her cheeks before she realised she was actually crying.

If there had been any doubts in her mind before of what she wanted, they were all gone now. She wanted her baby to have everything, not the material things but the real things in life that were important — and she knew that a daddy was one of those things.

The baby had a biological daddy, of course, but one who was involved in the most heinous crimes and Rebecca knew that she couldn't let her daughter be a part of that world in any way.

It seemed clear to Rebecca now that

blood ties were less important than a person who could love you, and that was what Rebecca saw in Will's eyes. He loved her baby, and she was beyond grateful for that. It didn't seem to matter in that moment whether he loved her too.

The baby was the most important person in her world and if Will was prepared to love her, then that would be enough for Rebecca.

'You're awake,' Will said very softly and for a moment Rebecca wasn't sure whether he was talking to her or the baby.

'How long have I been asleep?'

'About six hours.'

Rebecca couldn't believe she had slept that long, not when she had only spent minutes with her baby so far.

'Would you like to take over?' Will said. He was clearly loving every minute but as usual he seemed to know what Rebecca wanted and needed before she did.

'Please,' she said.

Will shifted forward and gently pulled the bottle from the baby's mouth, which formed a perfect O just before her face crumpled and she started to whimper. Will quickly placed her in her mother's arms and handed over the bottle. With the bottle back in its rightful place, the snuffling noises returned, and Rebecca marvelled at seeing her baby feed for the first time.

'She seems to have that all figured out,' Will said and he exchanged a smile with Rebecca.

'She's amazing,' Rebecca said and laughed at herself. 'Of course I may be a bit biased.'

'I think you're right,' Will grinned and gently swept a finger over the baby's forehead.

'She needs a name,' Rebecca said. 'I'm just not sure I can go with any of the ones that we . . . ' She couldn't finish.

'A new name. Peggy always said it didn't matter what you came up with before. You had to meet your baby before you could work out what their name truly was.'

Rebecca nodded thoughtfully.

'Do you have any suggestions?' Rebecca kept her eyes fixed on the baby, not sure she could risk seeing how he might react.

'Funny you should ask, but we — the baby and I, that is — thought that maybe Hope . . . '

Right at that moment, the baby opened her eyes and seemed to be in agreement with Will's idea.

Rebecca smiled. Perhaps they really had had a conversation to agree her name.

Hope hiccupped and Rebecca moved her forward in her arms so that she could rub her back. Hope let out a belch which didn't seem possible for a person of her size.

'That's settled it, then,' Rebecca said and smiled up at Will.

'Hope Buckingham, welcome to the world,' Will said with a big grin.

Hope seemed more interested in feeding than celebrating the fact that she now had a name.

'Is there any news?' Rebecca asked and looking up she caught Will's expression just as it turned serious.

'Nothing new,' he said.

If he hadn't have looked her straight in the eye, Rebecca would have sworn that he was hiding something from her.

'But it's early days in the investigation. They'll be looking at offences on home soil first, but my contact has assured me that if there's any connection with the Barter family then they will pursue it, even if it is simply handing over evidence to the British.'

Rebecca knew that was probably all she could have expected but she had wondered if it all might go away. It was a foolish dream, she realised, but it still made her sad that her life and Hope's would be so unsettled — for how long, she didn't know.

'I suppose I need to figure out where we should go now,' Rebecca said, mostly to herself.

'I have a suggestion, but there's no

pressure attached,' Will said.

'If you are offering to come with us . . . ' Rebecca shook her head. 'You've done so much for us already. I can't ask you to walk away from your life — especially when we have no idea how long you might have to be away.'

'That wasn't my suggestion,' Will said but despite his best efforts he sounded a little wounded at her reaction.

'Not that I'm not incredibly grateful for the offer,' she added quickly, but the words sounded hollow to her own ears and she almost wished she hadn't said anything as it seemed as if she was making it all worse.

'The immediate risk is over and with the FBI being involved I suspect the Barter family will think twice about sending someone after you again. So there's no reason why you and Hope couldn't come back to Blowing Rock.'

He didn't add 'with me' and Rebecca wasn't sure if he was thinking those words or not. Had her attempts to prevent him from entangling himself further in the mess that was her life sounded like a rebuff?

'At least there you would have people you can trust, who can help you. I've spoken to Peggy and she practically insisted.'

Rebecca could imagine the conversation but the fact that Will had felt the need to mention Peggy's insistence also made her heart drop a little. Perhaps it was the right thing to do, for Will's sake. She had no right to expect any more from him than she already had, not to mention the fact that she had just given birth to another man's baby. Perhaps if she really loved Will, then she should let him go. Her life would always be messy, even if the plan succeeded. Her baby's biological father was the favoured son of a crime boss and that was something neither of them would ever be able to completely escape. That was a lot for any man to take on — and Will had already been shot trying to protect them.

'What do you think?' Will asked.

Rebecca looked down at Hope, who had fallen asleep, still sucking on the bottle. It was almost empty so Rebecca teased it out of her tiny mouth. Hope sighed but continued to sleep.

'I think that sounds like a good option. As long as you don't mind?'

'Why would I mind?'

And Rebecca knew again that she had managed to hurt him, despite her best attempts to avoid any more hurt.

'I just thought you might have had enough. After all, since you met me you've had to flee your home, walk away from your job, been shot at and had to fight off a band of mercenaries — and you've barely known me two weeks!'

Rebecca tried to inject some humour into her voice but Will didn't return her smile.

'I gave you my word.'

Once again Rebecca had the distinct impression that she had managed to insult him.

What was happening? Now the

danger was less, they didn't seem able to have a conversation where they were both on the same page.

'I know — all I'm saying is I think you've gone above and beyond the call of duty.'

Rebecca searched his face, wanting him to read her emotions, as he had proven so good at doing, but she didn't see understanding there. Instead, what she saw was his cop face, unreadable and almost stern.

'The hospital want to keep us in for another couple of days. Peggy is going to drive up in her camper van and collect us. If that suits you?'

'That sounds perfect and very kind of her.'

'That's Peggy,' Will said. 'Well, if you can manage, I think I might go for a lie down.'

'Of course. You must be exhausted,' Rebecca said. 'Thank you for all you've done.'

Rebecca wasn't even sure if he had even heard her, as he wheeled his chair away faster than she would have thought possible.

Rebecca looked down at Hope who stirred and was now looking up at her through sleepy eyes.

'That my darling,' she said softly, 'is how to mess something up completely. There is a lesson there to leave difficult conversations until you have recovered from anaesthetic and operations.'

Rebecca's nurse returned then and gave her an encouraging smile that Rebecca thought probably meant she had heard at least some of the advice she had given her day-old baby.

'I think it's time you both got some sleep,' the nurse said, lifting Hope gently from her arms. She didn't want to put her down but she was feeling in desperate need of closing her eyes.

'I'll leave her in her cot here with you and I'll be right outside.'

Rebecca smiled her thanks. She knew it was normal for babies to be removed to the hospital nursery, but Rebecca didn't think she could bear the thought of Hope being taken away, not after everything that had happened, and her nurse seemed to understand that.

18

Rebecca was dressing Hope in a onesie that Peggy had brought up from Blowing Rock. It was nice to finally have Hope in clothes she could almost claim as her own. They had been donated by the lovely people from Will's home town and Rebecca was grateful once more for their generosity.

It was also good to be back on her feet.

Will had been helpful but detached and polite and she couldn't help but feel guilty that she had managed to hurt him. She had tried to talk to him about it but he always found a way to stop her in her tracks.

Rebecca leaned down and kissed Hope gently on the forehead. The baby blew her a bubble in return. Rebecca had never felt love like it. She couldn't imagine her life without Hope in it now, and that brought a fresh wave of guilt that James would not get the opportunity to know his daughter. But then, she reminded herself, he had made his choice — and he had chosen the family business over his unborn child.

She knew she would always wonder about that but she also knew it was too late. She knew she had made the right decision for Hope, but that didn't mean she didn't feel a mixture of emotions.

'We'll be all right, little one. Mummy's got this.' She went to scoop the baby up in her arms but Will seemed to appear from nowhere.

'No lifting, remember?' he said.

Rebecca felt a surge of anger but she knew she wasn't angry at Will. It wasn't his fault she had had to have a C-section and as a consequence wouldn't be carrying her own baby anywhere for at least six weeks. Peggy had insisted that both she and Will move in with her for a while until they were both back on their feet, so to speak.

Rebecca knew she wouldn't be able

to cope without help, but she wasn't sure how easy it was going to be to share a space with Will, since their relationship had regressed to polite and careful.

She also knew she couldn't expect Peggy not to look after Will — he was her eldest son, if not by blood then by choice.

Rebecca couldn't tell if Will was happy with the arrangements or not, but if she had to guess she would have gone with not.

'I was only going to lift her into the baby seat,' Rebecca said, gesturing to the seat that was resting on the side.

'You're three days post-op and you know what the doctor said.' Now Will sounded cross and that rankled Rebecca a little.

'Could you help me then, please?' Rebecca asked, trying to keep the frustration from her voice but thinking it was another thing she was failing miserably at.

Will said nothing but gently lifted Hope into his arms and then settled her into her seat, pulling the straps around her carefully and then tucking her in with a hand-knitted blanket from Peggy.

'I'll always help, Rebecca, you only have to ask — you know that.'

Will had said the words so softly that Rebecca wondered if she had imagined them.

'I know. I'm beyond grateful for your help.'

Will looked at her properly for the first time in days and he looked as if he was going to say something until Peggy bustled into the room, pushing a wheelchair.

'Are we ready to go? Will, where are your crutches? You aren't supposed to walk without them,' she chided.

Rebecca hid a smile at Will being told off.

'I'll get them and meet you at the car.'

'You'll get them and get taken to the exit in a wheelchair, like everyone else,' Peggy said in her no-nonsense tone.

'It's hospital policy,' she added as Will looked as if he was about to protest but then shrugged and limped from the room.

Rebecca eased herself into the wheelchair and an orderly appeared to carry the baby seat.

'Time to go home, girls,' Peggy said.

Rebecca felt a sudden influx of tears at the words. She wasn't sure if Hope would ever have a permanent home. She knew she would likely need to leave Blowing Rock at some point and that brought a fresh wave of pain. She swallowed hard. What she needed to do was focus on right now. That's what Hope needed her to do. There was no news from the FBI — and until there was, she wouldn't be able to make a decision.

*　*　*

Rebecca rocked the chair gently in the light from the small lamp. She was in the room Peggy had set up to be both her bedroom and Hope's nursery. Hope had woken just before four as she usually did, and Rebecca, despite her fatigue, cherished the moments they spent together.

In the dark, Rebecca could imagine how life could be different. Here in the safety of Peggy's house she could imagine a time when she and Hope could set up home and become part of a community, one they planned to be part of forever.

She had spent little time thinking about anything else. *Home*. It was something she had always striven for but never achieved. Rebecca had little family, and those that remained weren't particularly close. She had needed to make her own way in the world and so she had, constructing her own kind of family in her friends, but they were now all thousands of miles away. Her life in London felt as if it belonged to someone else. Even if the FBI could somehow miraculously deal with the Barter family, she couldn't imagine raising Hope in a city.

Here in Blowing Rock, with people that knew your name and cared enough about you to ask how you were, that was where Rebecca wanted to raise Hope. Surrounded by a community, in a place where people didn't bother to lock their doors, with green spaces everywhere and kids rode their bikes around town without a care.

Rebecca only allowed herself to imagine it was possible in the middle of the night, when she was alone. To do anything else, she knew, would just make leaving all the more difficult, and as the days went by with no news, any sense that it might be possible seemed to fade.

A gentle tap on her door brought her back to the here and now, and the reality of her situation.

'Come in,' she said softly, not wanting to disturb Hope who was falling asleep.

When the door opened, she expected to see Peggy, who would often wake with Hope and bring Rebecca a cup of herbal tea.

It was Will. His limp was barely noticeable now and he had ditched the crutches days ago.

'I saw the light on so I figured you were up,' he said softly and he glanced at Hope who was drifting back to sleep. 'I've had an update from Agent Creely and I thought you'd want to know.'

Rebecca shifted in the rocking chair and Will pulled over the ottoman and sat so he was near enough to speak quietly.

'The FBI passed their file on the Barter family to the British police and yesterday they undertook a series of raids.'

Rebecca felt as if all the breath had been squeezed from her lungs. She shook her head. Now that it was happening, she couldn't quite believe it.

'They arrested all the key players and are anticipating they'll all receive long jail sentences. Even when they're done, the FBI have a whole list of crimes committed in this country to add.'

'James?' Rebecca asked, her voice hoarse.

Will's expression shifted slightly. Rebecca couldn't tell if he was disappointed that she had asked about him or if he was worried how she would react to what he had to say.

'All the evidence points to James Barter being heavily involved in the illegal activities.'

Rebecca gasped and felt herself start to shake. Will reached a hand out for her shoulder.

'I'm so sorry, but Rebecca, we're talking modern slavery and drugs and all sorts of crimes against the vulnerable.'

Rebecca tried to speak through the sobs that were making her shake even harder but she couldn't. All she could do was fold herself into Will's arms.

When her sobs showed no sign of subsiding, Will lifted up her and Hope and sat himself in the rocking chair so that he could cradle both of them in his arms. He said nothing, merely rocked them back and forth, kissing Rebecca's hair.

'I'm so sorry, Rebecca. James was in

deep and there was no way to keep him out of it.'

'I know. It's almost a relief. When I left, I wasn't sure. I kept wondering if I had made a terrible mistake, that maybe with time, James might cut his ties with his family and come back to us.'

'You love him,' Will said. There was pain in his voice and Rebecca couldn't let him believe that any longer.

'No — I loved the man I thought he was. But everything he told me was a lie. All the time we were together he was involved in goodness knows what.' Rebecca shook her head. Hope started to whimper and she leaned down and kissed her.

'I can't change the fact that he's Hope's biological father but he will never be her daddy.' The words brought fresh tears to her eyes. 'I don't know how I'm going to explain it all to her.'

Rebecca felt a hand under her chin and Will gently lifted her face so that they were looking into each other's eyes.

'We'll tell her together,' he said.

That brought a fresh wave of sobs from Rebecca. 'I thought, after everything, you had decided we were too much trouble,' she sobbed.

Will's chest rumbled with a chuckle.

'I just wanted to give you some space. I had no idea what you wanted and I knew you needed to work through everything about James. If you aren't ready, I understand.' With an effort he kept his voice light. 'If you need time, I can give it to you. All I ask is that you stay here in Blowing Rock, you and Hope.'

Will reached an arm around so that he was cradling Hope too. Rebecca felt such a surge of emotion that she thought she would burst.

'I love you, Wilder,' she said. 'I think I have since the moment I saw you. I felt guilty about it. I had dragged you into the mess that was my life and then I was expecting you to love me back. I wanted to give you a way out. I thought you might just stay with us because you felt duty bound to.' Rebecca barely paused for breath during her little speech, she was so afraid that if she stopped she wouldn't be able to finish.

'Rebecca Buckingham, I love you, too, from the moment I saw you, but I felt I had no right to. You were clearly hurting so much from James and I couldn't add to your pain. But I couldn't bear to be apart from you. I hoped with time you might feel something for me . . .'

He kissed her and Rebecca responded. When they broke apart they were both a little breathless.

'I can assure you that nothing I feel for you has anything to do with honour and duty. I love you, Rebecca. I love you for your strength and for your single-mindedness.'

That last made Rebecca chuckle.

'OK — occasionally that gets a bit much, like when I saw you crawl through the cabin door.'

'I couldn't let them hurt you, and that was the only way I could think of to make them stop. After all you said they wouldn't hurt me,' she said, trying to make her actions sound more reasonable than they were in the cold light of day.

'That was quite a risk to take.'

'It was worth it,' Rebecca said, looking up at him. 'You know the Barter family thing may not be over. There's the trial and they have to be found guilty and even then, they may not be content to leave us alone . . .'

Rebecca had more to say but she was silenced with a kiss.

'Whatever happens, we'll face it together. You, me, and Hope. If you'll have me, that is.'

Rebecca had to lift a hand up to Will's face to check he was real. She knew she was grinning like a crazy person, but couldn't help it and at the same time she was crying — but for the first time in an age, these were happy tears.

'With all my heart,' she managed to say. 'If you'll have me and Hope.'

'There's nothing in this world I want

more — but there is one condition.'

Rebecca nodded; of course there would be. She couldn't expect Will to just take on everything. She was afraid of what he was going to say but knew she had to hear him out.

'Marry me,' he said.

Rebecca's mouth fell open. She couldn't believe what she had just heard.

'Wh . . . What did you say?'

'I said, will you marry me? That's my condition. I love you, Rebecca and I want to be with you forever. But I'm a traditional guy and when you find The One, that's what you do.'

'You really want to marry . . . me?' Rebecca's voice shook, and she still couldn't quite believe what she was hearing.

'I do,' Will said, and he gave her a half smile. 'I would get down on one knee but it's still a little dodgy.' He grinned. 'So, will you have me?'

Rebecca swallowed, she wanted to say the word but she couldn't so instead just nodded.

'Is that a yes?'

'Yes!' Rebecca finally managed to say, although in truth it was more of a shout.

Hope opened her eyes wide and they both turned their attention to soothing her.

'It's OK,' Will said, 'Mom and I are here.'

'Mummy and Daddy,' Rebecca corrected.

'Daddy? Are you sure?'

'I've never been more sure of anything in my life,' Rebecca said as Hope made a tiny fist around Will's finger. 'Clearly, neither has Hope.'

Rebecca could feel Will start to shake and she leaned closer into him. He was crying now, too and she felt him tighten his arms around her as she laid her head on his chest.

Epilogue

It was a simple ceremony, surrounded by friends and family. Marshall and Gaby had made the long journey from the perceived safe haven of their homestead. Even some of Rebecca's friends had come for the auspicious event.

'It is my great honour to tell you that you are now Hope Peggy Hayes,' the judge said, dressed in black robes but also wearing a broad smile.

'Does that mean Daddy is now my official daddy?' Hope asked solemnly.

She had turned five the day before and was wearing her best dress for the occasion.

'That's exactly what it means,' the judge said equally solemnly.

'Forever?'

'Forever and always,' Will said, lifting his daughter into his arms.

Will threw Hope in the air and she

laughed, the wholehearted giggle that only Will had ever been able to get out of her.

Rebecca looked on from her seat next to Peggy, jiggling ten-month-old Edward on her lap — named for Will's dad.

'Mommy!' Hope squealed, with one arm around her dad's neck and reaching out for her with the other. Rebecca got to her feet and Hope drew her and Teddy into a family hug.

'We're a real family!' Hope said in delight.

'We always have been, sweetheart,' Will said, kissing Hope affectionately on the forehead.

It had taken five years to finally convince James to let Will formally adopt Hope. Since James would be in prison until she was an adult, he had finally agreed it was for the best — and more importantly, it was what Hope wanted.

'I know,' Hope said smiling at Will. 'But now the judge has made it *law*.'

They all laughed.

Will and Rebecca had always been

open and honest with Hope but it had hurt both their hearts as they had watched her struggle to understand the choices James had made.

'Might I suggest a photograph to immortalise the happy moment?'

The judge had stepped down from his platform and was holding a rolled-up piece of paper, tied with a red ribbon. He handed it to Hope and she waved it in the air.

Marshall stepped forward and took a photo of the Hayes family, all together in love, forever.

We do hope that you have enjoyed reading this large print book.

Did you know that all of our titles are available for purchase?

We publish a wide range of high quality large print books including:
Romances, Mysteries, Classics
General Fiction
Non Fiction and Westerns

Special interest titles available in large print are:
The Little Oxford Dictionary
Music Book, Song Book
Hymn Book, Service Book

Also available from us courtesy of Oxford University Press:
Young Readers' Dictionary
(large print edition)
Young Readers' Thesaurus
(large print edition)

For further information or a free brochure, please contact us at:
Ulverscroft Large Print Books Ltd.,
The Green, Bradgate Road, Anstey,
Leicester, LE7 7FU, England.
Tel: (00 44) **0116 236 4325**
Fax: (00 44) **0116 234 0205**

A LITTLE BIT OF
CHRISTMAS MAGIC

Kirsty Ferry

As a wedding planner at Carrick Park Hotel, Ailsa McCormack is organising a Christmas Day wedding at the expense of her own holiday. Not that she minds. She's always been fascinated by the place and its past occupants; particularly the beautiful and tragic Ella Carrick, whose striking portrait still hangs at the top of the stairs. And then an encounter with a tall, handsome and strangely familiar man in the drawing room on Christmas Eve sets off a chain of events that transforms Ailsa's lonely Christmas into a magical occasion . . .

DOCTOR'S LEGACY

Phyllis Mallett

When Dr Helen Farley arrives in the Cornish fishing village of Tredporth as a locum, she feels instantly at home, and is fascinated by the large house standing on the cliffs. Owned by the ageing Edsel Ormond, her most important patient, the estate has two heirs: Howard and Fenton, Edsel's grandsons. But when Edsel informs Helen that he's decided to leave the property to Howard alone, on the condition that he first marries — and that the woman must be *her* — she realises her problems are only just beginning . . .

ROAD TO ROMANCE

Christine Lawson

A photography competition lands Penny Maxwell far from her job at the village bakery shop into the bright spotlight of fame. But she hasn't counted on the machinations of Robina Trent, who sees her likeness in the newspaper and realises they are virtual doubles. When Robina begins to make appearances in Penny's name, no one else is in on their secret. But little does Penny realise that loneliness and heartache will follow — for the man she loves, pianist Paul Hambledon, is stunned by the deep change in her . . .

ON THE MARRAM SHORE

June Davies

Catriona Dunbar is sent to stay with relatives on the Lancashire coast for the season. But between perpetually drunken Samuel Espley and his caddish son Julian, life in the grand house of Pelham is far from the happy holiday she had been anticipating. The only consolation is her growing friendship with the hired hand Morgan Chappel: a bond that seems poised to blossom into something more. Until Morgan is arrested — and Catriona must make a devil's bargain to save him . . .

NURSE CALEY OF CASUALTY

Quenna Tilbury

On Barbara Caley's first shift in Casualty, Damien Elridge, a film star, and his fiancée Margaret Knowles are brought in from a car accident. Damien has promised Margaret a part in a film, but an argument before the crash has put both that and their prospective marriage into doubt — and when Damien meets Barbara, he immediately expresses an interest in her. But Barbara is already in love with Adam Thorne, the Casualty Officer, who is also Margaret's ex-fiancé. Can the quartet find their way through the tangle to happiness?